About *A little brown sea*:

Because the story of a life is the story of the lives that intersect with it, *A little brown sea* broadens the scope of the novel to encompass the beings with which we share this planet and without which we cannot be fully ourselves. Charles Foster, working out in fiction the concerns that inform his remarkable non-fiction, combines here the curiosity of the scientist with the heart of a storyteller. I loved this aphoristic, argumentative and form-stretching novel, and hope others will let it mess with their heads.

Gregory Norminton

Charles Foster's *A little brown sea* is brilliantly original − a strange and elegant triumph.

Evie Wyld

The fragmented polyphony of Charles Foster's astonishingly ambitious and highly experimental debut novel, *A little brown sea*, expresses the essential *tohuwabohu* of the human condition and provides a vehicle for the exploration of 'ultimate questions' of meaning and purpose, particularly in relation to the human encounter with self and the natural world. The maverick spirit and boundary-breaking hybridity of the novel reflects similar qualities in Foster's celebrated philosophical enquiries *Being a Beast* and *Being a Human*, confirming him as one of the most singular and important — both playful and profound —voices of our time.

⸝ Ely

GW00759050

A LITTLE BROWN SEA

Charles Foster

For Vanessa and Alan,
with all good wishes.

Chas.

Fair Acre Press

First published in Great Britain in 2022 by Fair Acre Press
www.fairacrepress.co.uk

A CIP catalogue record for this book is available from
the British Library

ISBN 978-1-911048-70-1

Illustrations by James St.Clair Wade

Typeset by Nadia Kingsley

Cover design by Paul Kielty

CONTENTS

'The general view of [early] natural historians was that anything might exist in the sea…As more and more species were named and classified (often incorrectly), the tendency by the nineteenth century was to try to relate 'travellers' tales' to creatures already listed. The rapid growth of science gave it the intolerance of an adolescent, and the empiricism which had been one of the most praiseworthy features of the early writers went temporarily out of fashion….'

Gavin Maxwell, *Harpoon at a Venture*

PREFACE

I first met Theo, as I explain later, in a murmuring pub on the edge of the heaving brown sea of the Bristol Channel. It was a long way, in some ways, from the blue water of the Mediterranean that always heaved in him.

On paper we were quite similar, though his cv was much more brilliant than mine. We had paced some of the same cloisters, written for some of the same journals, admired some of the same women in the library and some of the same books - though his admiration, both of the women and the books, was far more nuanced than mine. We both liked mountains, seabirds, Mithraism, Arthurian legend and spoon-carving.

He seemed to be entirely without illusions. I had plenty.

When people asked me why I was writing this book I'd say: 'I've recently re-read *Moby Dick*. Melville says something along the lines of: "Unless you're thinking about and trying to write about the sea, you're contemptibly failing to confront the real issues of life." When I read that' (I'd say), 'I heard the slap of the gauntlet being thrown down, and felt I had to pick it up.'

It was meant to be an honest answer. But I've scoured *Moby Dick* for the quote, and it's not there. The nearest is this: 'But as in land-lessness alone resides the highest truth, shoreless, indefinite as God — so better is it to perish in that howling infinite, than be ingloriously dashed upon the lee, even if that were safety! For worm-like, then, *oh!* Who would craven crawl to land! Terrors of the terrible! is all this agony in vain? Take heart, take heart, O Bulkington! Bear thee grimly, demigod! Up from the spray of thy ocean-perishing — straight up, leaps thy apotheosis!'[1] Which is hardly the same thing.

The Greeks, the Jews and everyone else who bequeathed us our western memes, saw the sea as the end and the beginning: as a metaphor for chaos, destruction, and death, as well as for birth, re-birth, beauty and power.

The terrestrial Olympians didn't mess with Poseidon. They were very wise. But Yahweh, as we will see, won't cede jurisdiction over the sea, which makes for some interesting tensions.

There is a Chorus in this book. In ancient Greek drama the Chorus generally represents the voice of conservatism. It points out that no good will come of sleeping with your mother, and usually the play ends with the Chorus saying: 'Told you so'. Just occasionally the Chorus is confounded.[2]

There are also many non-human voices. I explain in the Author's Note why they're there, but I suggest you don't read that first.

Most of the book comes from drunken conversations with Theo, and from some notebooks of his that fell into my hands after … .well, later. I showed him very early drafts of some of the chapters. His comments were forthright and often angry. I've transcribed them as best I can.

I claim authorship because Theo hasn't, and because I doubt crows, dolphins or limpets will sue me.

You might think it's odd to have references in a book like this. But Theo and I are both in the academic business, and we'll never get out of the habit.

Charles Foster

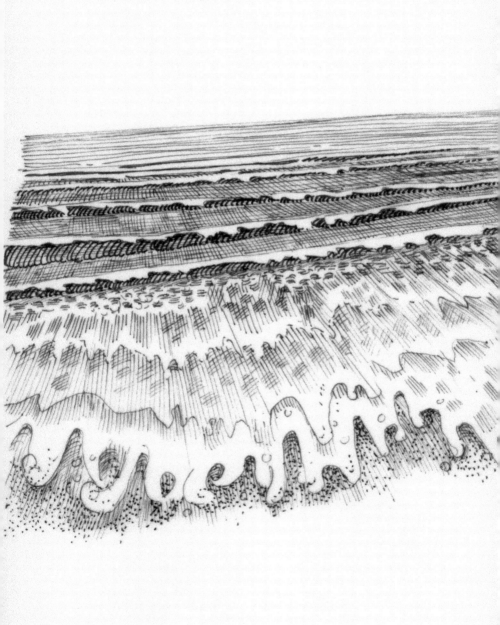

1. Clippings

The Western Weekly Argus and Courier, September 1, 2017

Police are investigating the disappearance of a Watchet man, Professor Theo Theotakis, who was last seen walking down High Street, Watchet, late on the evening of 25th August, having been with friends in The Ancient Mariner public house. He was expected to give a lecture at a meeting of the Minehead University of the Third Age on 27th August, but did not appear, having sent a note of apology to the organisers. Professor Theotakis is 48 years old, and described by police as 6 feet 1 inch tall, olive-skinned, and of slim build, with short-cropped black hair and a short black beard. He was wearing a green army pullover, a tweed jacket, brown trousers, and brown leather boots. Anyone who has any information should call Devon and Somerset police on…..'

He has a habit of playing with wooden worry-beads. He is understood to have been living alone outside Watchet, and to be an enthusiastic sailor.

Ken Millar, a close friend of Professor Theotakis, who was with him in The Ancient Mariner on 25th August, told the Argus: 'He's a great character, very clever and generous, and the life and soul of the party. He's a major contributor to local charities, and always has a kind word for everyone. When I saw him he seemed fine, although he was complaining a bit about a pain in his chest. But it eased off, and he was in good spirits. I appeal to anyone who has any information to contact the police. We are getting worried, and want him back!

A Textbook of General Surgery, Kung and Pinker, 2009

Sterile, biochemically inert foreign bodies generally present no threat, being usually walled off with fibrous tissue. But occasionally they can migrate and cause problems, in which case removal is mandatory.

www.mariguard.gr: October 29 2017

Forecast: Storm south of the Peloponnese at 1500 October 30. Wind speed at 9 Beaufort between Kythira and Crete. Waves in this area expected to be in excess of 12 metres. Greece's National Meteorological Service issued an updated weather warning at 1000 October 30. The warning is red.
This is the highest level. Citizens and authorities are advised to take urgent precautionary measures.

www.mariguard.gr: October 31 2017

The expected storm off the Peloponnese 'did not materialise', a source at the Greek National Meteorological Service said today. 'We will continue to monitor the situation', the spokesman continued, 'and urge citizens and authorities to remain vigilant.'

Yeni Ayna ('New Mirror') newspaper, Istanbul: October 30 2017

Major storms in the southern Aegean have caused significant loss of life, sources report. A Panamanian-registered freighter ran aground off Thera (Santorini), with the loss of all crew and cargo (said to be cars and commercial vehicles destined for Beirut). Several smaller vessels were reported missing. Three children were washed into the sea in Amorgos, and another two in Naxos. No bad weather warnings had been issued by the Greek authorities.

Bulletin of the Andalusian Natural History Society: December 2017

In September and October there were numerous reports, from throughout our region, of gannets (Morus bassanus) flying east. Sightings were mostly far offshore, but a group of five birds (including four juveniles) were seen feeding in the Golfo de Almeria. Bryan Nelson ('The Atlantic Gannet', 2002), speculates that it is easier for inexperienced immature birds to feed in the winter in the calmer waters of the Mediterranean than in the more challenging Atlantic (where most of the adults are to be found).'

Φαλαμβουρι (Phalambouri) newspaper, Athens: 5 January 2018

Turkish authorities continue to deny any knowledge of the body of a UK citizen, allegedly washed ashore near Marmaris. Tourists spotted coastguards removing a corpse last Tuesday. It was apparently badly decomposed, but one onlooker insisted that it was clearly the body of a woman. The source of the rumour that the body was that of a UK citizen is unclear, but may be the UK Embassy in Ankara, who over recent weeks have sought information about a boat, crewed by at least one Briton, which was spotted in the Ionian Sea in the autumn.

2. Beginnings

Author

This story started in a pub on the edge of a little brown sea in the English West Country. I've always been happy there. They serve farm cider, pressed through straw, with smiling approval, and industrial lager, pressed through a polyurethane nozzle, with undisguised contempt.

No, that's not right. It started when Archbishop Makarios III of Cyprus was deposed by the military junta in Athens, and replaced by Nikos Sampson, leading to the Turks invading Cyprus on 20 July 1974.

But no, that's not right either. It started when John, sitting in a cave on Patmos (the nearest Greece gets to a dour, Presbyterian island), looked out at the porpoises playing and prophesied that when the Son of Man finally triumphed, there would be no more sea.[3]

It was the culmination of many old Jewish dreams. The ocean was chaos and death. Leviathan, its most representative inhabitant, was God's opponent. Jesus established his credentials with skeptical Jews by stilling the lurching sea, and his followers, holding his hand, went through the waters of death onto the dry land of the New Creation. God speaks to his people from the top of desert mountains. The sea's no home for decent folk. Only fornicators with tarry pigtails live there.

But no: It started when my ancestors, and those of Archbishop Makarios and Nikos Sampson, hauled themselves out of the sea on their fins and then, wondering what they were, and from where they'd come, looked back at the sea and said: 'that's home'. We never left, in fact. Along with all mammals, we start off in our own sea: a warm bag of amniotic fluid, with its own tides.

Old people pay good money to look out at an amniotic sea from the windows of their retirement home, as if there's some sort of promise of rebirth.

Home: not home: a dissonance that makes it impossible for us to rest.

Yet my biological beginning is no beginning either. Genesis agrees with all modern scientists that water creatures came before the land creatures.[4] But the waters were there *before* the beginning: before the heavens and the earth. 'In the beginning, God created the heavens and the earth….The earth was without form and void, and darkness was over the face of the deep.'[5]

The earth and the waters were distinct. It was the earth that was created. The waters pre-existed. 'And the Spirit of God was hovering over the face of the waters.' Not over the earth, mark you. If you want to know God, go to the waters. He's still hovering there.

All of which is to say that a book about the sea is bound to fail. If you can't even attempt an account of origins, you're more or less bound to get everything else wrong. An argument is only as good as its premises. If you don't have any premises, you're doomed to incoherence and futility.

Go back to the bookshop and ask for a refund.

ΨΨΨ

If they wouldn't give you the refund, and you're stuck with this, we should try to start with some facts.

That's not so easy.

But let's say, tentatively, that:

(1) There is a pub by a harbour in the English West Country.
(2) Until a few years ago, at the corner of the bar of this pub, a Greek Cypriot called Theo was typically to be found between the hours of 6 and 11 p.m.
(3) Between his shoulder blades there was, or is, a puckered scar.
(4) He lived in a hut in a cluster of trees on a tiny island, three miles from the pub. The island is joined to the mainland at low tide by a strip of rock. To this day there are no other human inhabitants.
(5) Two hundred miles away, in an old university, there is a room looking out over a tidy quadrangle to a mediaeval chapel. To the despair of the domestic bursar, the room smells incurably of liturgical incense.

And here are some of the characters:

The sea: whose origins and nature have been mentioned already.

Theo Theotakis (Homo sapiens): A Greek-Cypriot boy who became a rather Greek man. As a man, a professional philosopher, until he repented of it.

Short-beaked Common Dolphin (Dolphin delphis): born off Skye, within sight of the Cuillin ridge. Got stuck on his way out from his mother, and was pulled out by an aunt, whose tooth marks can still be seen by his pectoral fins.

He has an Encephalization Quotient (EQ) of five, which means that the ratio of his brain weight to his body weight is five times the average for mammals, which, if you take such crude indices seriously, means that he's a lot smarter than a chimp (EQ = 2.3).[6]

You'd expect an animal with a brain that big to be highly relational, to have a good memory, to need entertainment, to be comfortable with abstractions, and to seek pleasure for pleasure's sake.[7] All this is true of him.

***Carrion Crow (Corvus corone)*:** hatched in a basket of sticks, bones and rabbit sinews swaying at the top of a beech tree on the cusp of moor, meadow and sea, somewhere in Somerset. Female.

***Gannet (Morus bassanus)*:** one of the flecks of summer snow covering Grassholm, off the Pembrokeshire coast: a savage island of scaly Jurassic feet and cold blue eyes with black pupils, set in a murderous tidal race. One of the only places on earth where, moment by moment, you can smell natural selection. Governed by stern equations and slim margins. Also female.

***Herring gull (Larus argentatus)*:** hatched on a chimney a few doors down from the pub. Drifted down to Cornwall in search of fish guts and ice cream. Caught in a winter storm which bundled him up in a parcel of Newfoundland air, took him back to the pub and slammed him into a corrugated iron barn just behind the gents.

***Rachel (Homo sapiens)*:** a human female, aged six when she met Theo.

She is a very close relation of Archbishop Makarios III, Nikos Sampson, all the Turkish troops who invaded Cyprus, and Theo, and a close relation of the dolphin, the carrion crow, the gannet, the herring gull, and the eel we'll meet in a moment.

Her original home (where her ancestors first became *Homo sapiens*) is on the plains of East Africa, which is why, if she gets a garden in England, she's likely to want trees that look like acacias, with low branches that will let her escape easily from lions.[8]

It's why, too, she feels more comfortable when she can see big, sa-vanna-like vistas, and why she likes fires and birdsong. At some point, though, her ancestors may well have spent some time at the seaside. There, from shellfish and other marine life, they may have got the essential fatty acids and iodine necessary for building her enormous brain.[9] She has an EQ of 7.6, but much prefers stories to arithmetic.

For most of the time she is an Upper Palaeolithic child. Most mod-ern children are. Three quarters of our history as behaviourally mod-ern humans is Upper Palaeolithic, and though modernity has done its diabolical best to rob us of that glorious inheritance, by and large, except in open-plan offices, it has failed). And so Rachel likes sugar and living in trees and holes. She has no sense of dominion over the natural world. A hedgehog is a brother, but brothers sometimes have to be eaten if the ice-sheets come too close. She is urgently concerned with tribal hierarchies. She has five siblings, and she watches very carefully to see that they don't get more than their share of the kill, or a place too close to the fire.

She is my daughter. I love her to distraction, and would die to save her even if I knew she was sterile. Darwin wouldn't like that.[10]

Most of her sensory receptors are buried in her head, and her head is much closer to the ground (and thus to her non-human cousins) than is mine. For her, a leaf is a leaf, not an idea of a leaf. It is to be understood as fully as possible, using all the available sensory tools. There is no reducing valve in her brain, slowing the stream of sen-sation to the manageable dribble that we call 'real life'. She's never been told that it is better to look and think than sniff and lick.

Until very recently she was barely a biped. Her hands as well as her feet told her about the ground from which she'd come, and to which she must return.

She likes junk films just as she likes sugar, and for the same atavistic reasons: you get something for minimal effort, even if, these days, it kills you.

Eel (*Anguilla anguilla*): This eel's mother had spent a happy century in an Italian river. She had long known that it could not last. The time came. Her ovaries swelled and her gut withered. Burning the fat of the season's worms, bullheads and ducklings, she made her trip to the weed-sea off Bermuda where all eels begin and end. [11] She entwined for a few frantic minutes with a small male from Morocco. Spent, they spiralled down to the sea bed to be eaten. That was a century before our eel enters this story.[12] While her parents were still spiralling, our eel, along with millions of other larval eels, started to drift towards Europe.

Wedged between two layers of water of slightly different temperatures and salinities, the larval daughter floated north-east for a few years. A year away from Somerset there was a jolt from some sort of weird field, and she started to change into a transparent swimming thing.

Through her body, past her heart and gut, you could see, if you were down there in the cold, the old eyes of sharks, the newer fins of whales, plastic bags from Venezuela and tampon applicators from Miami.

When she reached England she knew she had to go up, up: to get away from the salt that meant both birth and death: to feel the brown water always bearing down, down into the face. She acquired pigment, locality and habits.

It would have been kind to give eyelids to all eels and all other fish. Instead they rinse their eyes constantly in water. If they had eyelids we'd credit them with expression and soul, and wouldn't kill them as casually as we swat flies.[13]

This eel, though she couldn't hint at it by winking delight or balefulness, valued her life.

She recognized hundreds of individuals and knew that they, like her, had history. As a youngster she liked the dark lee of an Exmoor river near a spot where criminals had been gibbeted – not because it was particularly safe or the hunting particularly good (no maggots had dropped from highwaymen's corpses for a while) – but simply because, for a few decades, it was *home*. In her late middle age she came to like the smell of the salt mud of the River Parrett, clotted though it is with diesel oil and cadmium because…well, because she liked it.

And now, an old lady, she had come back to the meeting of the land and the sea. She liked to bury herself tail-down in the mud, her head sticking into the water like a candle on a satanic birthday cake; snapping at baby dabs a tree's length from Theo's hut.

At some level she knows that when she next goes properly to sea it will be to spawn and die. Perhaps she will choose when to hit puberty, and so go to sea, and so when to die, or perhaps she will feel the swell of her tyrannous ovaries inside her, as we feel the pressure of birthdays and the slowing of our legs.

Various others, to be introduced as they appear. Since they all exist today, and have a common origin, they are all the product of exactly the same amount of evolution. A limpet cannot boast that its roots are longer than a banker's, or that it has been worked more carefully by the attrition of tide, beak, tooth, and sexual rejection.

3. July 1974

The Author

At midday a boy was fishing, knee deep, in a purring sea.

His mother, too pretty for her own good, watched him from a grove of silver-leafed olives shimmering in the hot wind from Africa like sardines.

The boy hooked a fish, wound it up through the foothills of under-sea mountains, wrenched the hook from its eye, and turned round to wave to his mother – a wave that said that he was at the top of life's pyramid, and could look after her now.

But his mother was looking inland. The field behind was growling.

A lorry-load of sweating, spotty boys in khaki was bumping towards the house, bristling with bayonets.

The mother crossed herself and ran inside to fetch an old shotgun, meant for pigeons and suicide. She pushed a cartridge into the breach, ran outside, and mouthed to the boy: 'They're here!' He stood for a moment, and then started to run through the surf and up the beach.

He saw the lorry jolt to a halt beside the house. As the soldier-boys jumped out, his mother lifted the gun to her shoulder, took aim at the leader, and pulled the trigger.

Nothing happened.

A rifle butt burst her face. She was dragged inside. The whole truck load followed, but one of them turned at the door and saw the boy. The boy ran. So did the soldier. The boy ran back to the sea. There was a cave, reached by swimming through an underwater rock door, where they'd never find him.

He never got there. A gun rattled at the same rate as the cicadas.

A single bullet, 7.92 x 57 mm Mauser, lead core with a hard metal jacket, thumped into the boy's back.

I have a deactivated Mauser round on my desk as I write. It is a beautiful, biological thing, built like a swallow's wing to reduce the drag from thyme-scented air and the wobble from the heat between cypresses.

The boy slumped forward into a wave. Water spun into the bullet hole (going clockwise, since Cyprus is in the northern hemisphere).[14] It bent in with it a fold of the sea's pelt: a glutinous film of filth and wriggling things. As he lost consciousness his own skin nipped off the fold, which spiraled down into his chest and wound round the bullet. Along with the sea-hide went the breath of a Loggerhead turtle and a plesiosaur, the blowing of a whale, a couple of particles of a Minoan urn, some bone from the sternum of a Trojan princess, and a cocktail of sewage from Alexandria and Tripoli (and thus wine from the Atlas and rice from the Nile Delta).

The soldier, appalled by what he'd done, pulled the boy out onto the tideline, vomited over him, was appalled at that, and ran back to the house, determined to restore his manhood.

ΨΨΨ

For a week the boy was synaesthetic. The surgical spirit smelt blue; the water they spooned into him tasted black. The pain, as they probed the wound and flushed out the whale spurt, was lush and green. He heard the faces, as they bent over him, as tinklings.

They gave him ketamine for some procedure, forgetting the amnesiac drug that normally goes with it, and he rose out of his body, looking down from six feet above the operating table, watching with interest as the surgeons worked, and thinking how shocked his mother would be that no one had dusted the top of the cupboard over which he hovered.[15] He was too tired to be disappointed when his clumping mule of a body waved a hoof and beckoned him back into himself.

Somehow his father was there, weeping and stroking and clutching and smelling of himself and sheep and lemons rather than of a colour.

Somehow, too, some time, the boy was in the belly of a boat, his father beside him again, smelling now of sweat and oil.

A chain clanked up. The boy heard the rust, the weed, the wrench of rock, the scurrying of fish and the languid comment of an octopus, and then the boat swung round, bellowed, and snorted its way towards Gibraltar.

Yelkouan Shearwater (*Puffinus yelkouan*)

The shearwater had come to the island along a deep valley of scent that had begun off the coast of Syria, meandered down past Haifa, and then turned north. Sometimes the valley had closed around the bird like a barrelling wave. The bird knew the valley well; it had followed older tubenoses up and over the olfactory crag between Sicily and Tunis; along the furrow from Alexandria to Port Said, and had flown into the valley one cold afternoon when it was glutinous with squid. It rarely left now: it knew the hollows, the high tops, and the contours of the walls. But the winds of the last week had deranged the valley, as burglars might sling around furniture, and the bird felt it should go away until the world had sorted itself out. It had skirted Cyprus, finding only useless dry, spiky resins. But that day it had got something else - faint but unmistakable. A plume of dead sea things, a hundred feet high, streaming from a hot field. The bird was right, but there was nothing in it for him. The scent was unlocked from the bodies of Carboniferous animals sucked out of Arabia; from the exploding diesel of the truck.

The mother's yelps reminded the bird of the gulls that waited outside the burrow in Malta where it was hatched. It jerked away towards Syria.

Theo

My mother was killed in the Turkish invasion of Cyprus in 1974. I was injured. I was five at the time. I left with my father shortly afterwards. We were taken in by some of my mother's family who ran a Greek restaurant in Sheffield.

Chorus

It is not quite as simple as that.

Sheffield, by one method of calculation, is a long way from the sea. By other methods it is not so far.

4. A Greek child

vvvvvvvvvvvvvvvvvvvvvvvvvvvvvvvvvvvvvvvvvvvvvvvvvvvvvv

The Author

Theo's father, so that no one could think he was being parasitic on the family, found a job as a clerk in an insurance company.

He was always the first to arrive and the last to leave, which meant that from the age of five Theo had to find his own way to and from school and amuse himself until supper time.

The father was indispensable and never promoted.

Theo was always immaculately turned out. His shorts had knife-edge creases, you could see his big moon face in the toecaps of his old-fashioned shoes, and every other day he was hanged at his nice, middle-class school with the tie he always wore.

Apart from the hangings, he was invisible and inaudible. No one remarked on his accent or on the way his black hair stood stiffly to attention.

He rose silently and unapplauded - both at school and at home - from the bottom to the top of the class.

His English was formal, precise, archaic and technical – a bequest from the old pre-supper *Encyclopaedia Britannia*. His mathematics were wonderful and prematurely creative. His geography was largely drafted by a British colonial administrator and supported by redundant statistics about jute yields and ivory imports. But though London was the centre of the visible world, Athens was the hub of all invisible worlds worth inhabiting.

After a terse audit of the day's marks and grades, Theo and his father ate supper in silence. His mother presided. A place was always set for her, and her photo was at the head of the table. The dead are companionably present at every Greek table. They stare monochromally out in stiff collars or poplin frocks, checking that everyone's eating up, frowning on insolence and inappetance, smiling as the wine goes down, but deferring to the living, knowing that shades can only give the broadest, most generic advice to those in the sun.

Theo's mother was different. She couldn't accept her own death. She hadn't gone quietly, and never would. The minutiae of the day were her business. She determined how much salt should go in the greens, what brand of oil to buy, Theo's bed time, whether to say the prayers in a confident or deferential tone, and what presents should be bought for the cousins. The father's only known conversations were by way of constant, muttering séance.

When they saw the family, the father's courtesies were grave and impeccable, but never led to the chaffing, hand-waving, eye-rolling hyperbolae for which they had been designed by generations of Greeks. There were sacred rules of engagement, but no engagement. There was nothing to discuss. All was clear.

Nor was there anything to celebrate. The father's continued existence and his Greekness were facts: they needed only to be acknowledged. Greeks clink glasses before they drink wine or tsipouro because wine and tsipouro, like the world they enhance, must be experienced in all sensory modalities: they have to make a noise as well as tasting and smelling of something. But Theo's father clinked glasses only to acknowledge that one clinked glasses.

The father didn't refuse promotion out of humility. Quite the opposite. He knew what he was and where he was from. He was a Greek, and therefore a philosopher. No philosopher would confuse identity and function. Being an insurance clerk was simply what he *did*.

Greek philosophers, needless to say, were in all respects better than Yorkshire insurance clerks. The father didn't despise the other clerks: they had a part to play. He would write about them one day, taxonomically. He would count their legs and describe the markings on their abdomens.

At the Greek Orthodox Church every Sunday morning Theo learned, after the manner of apophatic theology, what God was not. 'What is God?', a black-cassocked priest would ask. 'He is not A. Nor B. Nor even, though it is tempting to think so, C. And what is He like? He is like nothing. Nothing, that is, except Himself. Remember His declaration? 'I am whom I am.'"

This pleased Theo very much. He saw that it did not follow from God's incomprehensibility that God made no comprehensible demands. Indeed, he wondered, perhaps the fact that moral demands emerged from an incomprehensible source was what made them truly moral and truly demanding. He felt the eyes of the icons on him, and knew that the dead were alive and participating. They showed him their suffering and glory and dared him to disbelieve.

The rule of the dead was confirmed by the naïve genetic determinism of the age, speaking through Theo's mousy biology teacher, Miss Birch.

'Now listen, children. You are made of protein. Your genes, which you got from your ancestors, determine what sort of proteins you have, and so what you are. Any questions?'

That evening, over the meatballs, his father looked at the presiding photo for confirmation, and said: 'Miss Birch might be protein,

Theo, but you are the son of Agamemnon and Achilles'. Which seemed to Theo to confirm what Miss Birch had said. Anyway, whether he was shaped by nature or nurture, Theo knew that he was created wholly by the dead. His DNA came from the grave, and so did his environment.

ΨΨΨ

There were two windows in Theo's bedroom. One looked out over the polite row of semi-detached houses on the other side of the road, each with its drive, its polished car and its roses and hydrangeas caged in privet.

The other looked out, when it was light, to small steep fields carved up by drystone walls, and beyond them, suspended from the sky rather than rising from the land, heather moorland, cackling with grouse. When it was dark the fields vanished, and instead the wild window was filled with Time: usually the Neolithic or before: circles of stone: puddles of blood: birds that *knew*.

In the in-between times, when Space became Time at dusk, and Time became Space at dawn, a white owl flapped along the seams, killing things from one side or the other.

One day the owl was hit by a car. Theo found it by a bus stop.

That night, and ever after, his back window showed only a darkened version of the day. The owl's weaving flight had stitched the past and the present together. With its death the past, always elastic, had retracted beyond sight.

The nighttime fields were now filled with rabbits and voles rather than with Time and, hunting them, foxes that arrived there when the last ice sheets retreated. The foxes lived under sheds in gardens like Theo's, and chose (out of simple racial pride and the need for entertainment) to kill, though they could have survived effortlessly on curry and pizza from dustbins. They watched TV through the gaps in curtains, though their brains would still have infallibly and immediately have registered 'Wolf!' or 'Mammoth!' had one slunk or lumbered up past the newsagent.

The foxes used all their senses all the time. They, like Theo might have been, were splendid sensory all-rounders – not olfactory specialists like the badgers which lived in the corner of the cemetery and ate earthworms that had eaten bank managers; or visual and auditory experts like the smashed owl.

The foxes, like Theo, had wonderful eyes, noses, ears, and absurdly sensitive feet. Many types of data streamed into those sharp red heads from fields and playgrounds and gardens. The world built by their heads was much more like (or much less unlike) the real world than the worlds of the badger, the owl, or Theo. If he had known how to follow them, the foxes could have shown Theo what his home was like. Theo could then have started to live in that home, rather than in a pastiche of it.

Fox (*Vulpes vulpes*)

A dog fox sat in the roses and looked through the window. It saw a grizzled man and a cub. They were still. The man was not playing with the cub, or feeding it, or yapping at it. They both looked as if they were going to die. This was not surprising, because the smell of astringent poison came from the room. It was dreadful; it crushed out all other sensation. It is this poison that is killing them and making them so quiet, thought the fox. If they do die I wouldn't want to eat them. And so it walked off.

The Author

Some other children didn't need the foxes' help. They burrowed into the tip behind the school and made nests at the top of trees and rafts to sail to Zululand. They shot at rabbits with bows and arrows and, when they missed them, consoled themselves by roasting road-kill squirrels and making loin-cloths from the skins. The occasional Yorkshire sun didn't burn them because they were coated with mud from the dam by the café. They knew the minds of ant columns, gave pet names to the solitary bees, dissected owl pellets, and were infested by hedgehog fleas. They had bird skulls strung talismanically round their necks, bird tongues and moths in matchboxes by their beds, and bracken in their pillows.

That is: they knew that they were part of a grand scheme: a huge, pulsing, constantly moving system, and they began to know what sort of creatures they were themselves.

They knew too where they were and *when* they were. They knew that they were balanced on the edge of the gritstone and the limestone, that the martins arrived a few days after they'd been seen in Dover, that there had been a wreck of Little Auks on the Moor some time in the 1930s and that the auks had brought with them a cargo of fish parasites from the seas off Spitsbergen, that the Pennines began at the back of the farm in Edale where they all went camping, and that the wind came from the west - which meant that the city's effluent was dumped on the poor people to the east, which didn't seem right, though the poor people never seemed to mind much.

The kids knew that the flat vowels and the flat caps meant they were in the north, and that the snow would lie for a month longer in Porter Clough and Wyming Brook than it would in Bluebell Wood, and two months longer in Bluebell Wood than it would in London.

When the swallows arrived they celebrated with Falstaffian draughts of Dandelion and Burdock. They knew that a drop of house martin dung had many molecules in it from the forest and veldt of Africa. They knew that in the corner where the TV now stood, not so long ago there had been a real sabre-toothed tiger.

When they couldn't be outside, they got the bus to the museum, where they knew the expressions of all the stuffed animals. A squint-eyed woodcock looked confused; a pine marten arrogant. All the animals had been impeccably mothproofed, and were therefore immortal and therefore sanctified. All other animals participated in this sanctity.

But, most distinctively, they were the kids of the Edge. Suddenly the privet hedges ended. Suddenly there was the wild. They didn't bleed into one another.

You might think that this would produce amphibians, flopping happily between the two worlds. It didn't. It posed a stern question: to which nation do you belong? Most of them never hesitated. The offer of wild nationality never lapsed, but most who took it took it early.

These children (the children of teachers, physicists and steel magnates) were kinder than the rest. By and large they remained kind. Many of them stayed in Sheffield to climb rocks, run through heather, do small mammal surveys and make beer from brown moor-water. The few who sold mortgages or became ad execs carried with them a gnawing remorse that sometimes saved them.

Theo watched them with a pure hot lust he later sublimated into a passion for mathematical proofs, and an envy he later felt for mothers pushing buggies in the park. He saw the kindness, and saw where it came from. But though he flirted with the children, he could not follow them, or learn from the foxes. Why? Well, this was the reasoning, as articulated by his father:

1. Turks are wild.
2. We are not Turks.
3. Therefore we are not wild.

There was a gentler form, which came from the rest of the family:

1. We are Greeks.
2. Greeks gave civilization to the world.
3. Civilization and wildness are enemies.
4. Therefore to be Greek is to be an enemy of the wild.

Both were versions of the Jewish justification for circumcision. Why hack off foreskins? Because it is unnatural. The Canaanites (our enemies: the *not-us*) are tragically natural. They have exuberant foreskins. To be natural is to be uncivilized: un-anointed: un-special. We'll declare in the flesh our difference from them.

In the Jewish iteration the argument and the act became central to identity and psychology. In its Greek form, the argument is the sort of self-parody only sustainable in a precarious diaspora community. No Greek living in Greece could ever have uttered it. You'd know it was nonsense whenever the wind from Hymettus blew through the toilet. But banality has its own power. Until his balls dropped, Theo was completely convinced by the argument.

So, until they dropped, bringing Dionysus down to Sheffield with them, Theo lived in a deadly world of detergent, Brillo pads, mothballs, herbicide, mouse-traps, ironing-boards, medicated tissues, self-help manuals, Readers' Digest abridgements and punctual bed times.

Bacteria were proxies for the Turks. To resist ignorance was to resist Turkish landing craft. To populate a head with facts was to man a fort. To press a crease into a shirt was to assert a national boundary.

You could spot a quisling at twenty paces because his shoes didn't shine and his nose wasn't wiped.

If he'd asked them, the wild kids would have taken Theo to their own Hymettus behind the dam: shown him dryads and satyrs: taught him, through the tawny owl in the elm on the school field, the international language of owls - which is the language of Athena herself. But by the time Theo got to know the wild kids well, he was at war, and didn't have the time.

For when Theo was thirteen, wildness, and hence Turkishness, started to erupt all over his body and, worse, in his head. It seemed that the ironing and abridgements had failed. The enemy was within the gates. It seized him and shook him and distributed the 'him' so widely and thinly between the parts of his life and his psyche and his stained sheets that he couldn't point to anywhere, at any time, that *he* clearly was.

The wild kids knew where and what they were. They always had known. They were where, and what, they had always been. No hormonal tides could shift them. They had long known that fertilization happened in the gardens, moors and woods where they were, and it wasn't very surprising that it could happen to or from the kids themselves. If you know that you are X, and he is Y and not X, X and Y can relate. If you know what you are you can bring yourself to meet Y at the appointed time at the street corner to go to the cinema. So they had real relationships, with emotion and responsibility rather than grunt and spurt. It's said they still do.

Even if Theo had been able to identify himself for a moment, there would have been no obvious continuity between him and the entity that had occupied the earlier, hairless edition of his body. An endocrinological midwife had tugged into the world a new creature of unknown parentage.

Births are usually marked by some sort of ceremony. The baby's head is wetted; there's a cake each year. But the birth of the pubescent 'Theo' (as we'll call him for convenience' sake) was not even mentioned in his house. Worse, it was unmentionable. In wise cultures he'd have been taken into a wood, painted, cut, made to fast and kill, to watch a branch sleeplessly for three days and three nights, taken to talk with his dead grandfather, and brought back on hunters' shoulders.

In Sheffield there was an increase in pocket money and parental suspicion, and a giggling talk about ejaculation from the mortified Miss Birch, who'd looked it up the night before.

The new wildness of the pubescent body is bad enough for regular kids. For Theo — and particularly because of the wild kids he so admired - it was terrible. Not only did he not have a self (and it was tricky to be a good Greek if you weren't even a person), but that not-self had to bear the guilt of familial, national and historical betrayal. In having unquellable tides of unexaminable and unspeakable passion boiling through him, and in admiring the wild kids, he'd opened the door to the old enemies. The deaths in the pass at Thermopylae had been in vain. He'd redrawn the boundary of Macedonia. He'd tortured and re-killed his sainted mother.

Theo's father, disgusted and despairing at the monosyllabic Turk diffused through the house and defying the deodorant, put Theo — then aged fifteen - on a flight to Athens.

ΨΨΨ

He was met at the airport by a large, well-briefed, and improbably Greek uncle and gripped by huge hairy hands, built for wringing out doubt and throttling Turks. They marched manfully to the blue and white striped car. The uncle's *komboloi*[16] clicked belligerently to the rhythm of his hot Aegean heart, built from roast lamb and swollen with love of country. Rebetiko croaked out of the cassette player; martyred Byzantine virgins looked impassively at the luggage, which secreted, tucked inside the *Odyssey*, a samizdat copy of the good bits from *Lady Chatterley*.

The road into Athens, boomed the uncle, was a wonder of modern engineering. Its camber was revolutionary, its tarmac innovative, its bridges immune to the worst earthquakes. The concrete of Athens' buildings showed unusual elasticity and salt-resistance. The food quivered with vitamins, the air was honeyed wine, and only the very evil could die. And the maidens of Athens, Theo was told in excruciating, whiskery confidences, were – well - beyond the praise even of the exquisite Greek language. 'Their *hips*, young man…' breathed the uncle, before words finally failed him.

Words, meanwhile, which had long failed Theo, were returning to him with an Anglo-Saxon pungency. But for three long weeks he stared mute at the wonders of the Periclean Age, and at plates of taramasalata and mountain greens, and at the gyrations of wedding guests (*'Those* hips, Theo: splendid examples of their kind'), and at the night, biting his tongue until he dribbled blood into his wispy non-beard. Then he snapped.

The snap involved going to a dusty bookshop off Monastiraki and buying a bird book.

ѰѰѰ

It was too late. The wild kids had moved on, together. They had left the Edge behind for him, but for Theo it wasn't just the edge of the herbaceous border. It was an embattled border, remember. It took years for him to see it without soldiers, and to hear Long-Eared owls rather than the click of stamps on passports.

That Greek trip left one mark. One afternoon, walking alone through the olive groves on the Acropolis, eating baklava and looking for tortoises, Theo saw a stone in the famous Hellenic light: light which made context irrelevant and turned *a* stone into *the* stone: the stone by which all stones were judged. It wasn't a stone, but the model of *stone-ness*.

He stopped, transfixed. He was a moth pinned to a cork board. Syrup ran down his hand and urine down his leg. His cheeks felt as if they had brushed against the fur coats in the wardrobe on the way into Narnia. He sank to the ground, but his eyes never left the rock. Compared to the rock he was froth. The rock was infinitely heavy: he weighed barely as much as his breath.

This sort of experience is, of course, so routine a part of childhood – part of the web and weave of all children other than those abused by screens and sofas – that it would hardly be worth mentioning but for one thing: the time when it happened. Theo was a very late developer.

'The spell was only broken', he wrote in his diary that night, 'when I heard the hooting of a tourist bus.' That was wrong. I hesitate to say it was dishonest. His real conviction, then and thereafter, was that his life before the stone, and most of his life afterwards, was the stuff of spell, delusion, distortion and truncation. Only on the Acropolis, a few hundred yards from where Plato had preached the Theory of Forms[17] (no doubt after a similar epiphany), was he free of the malignant enchantment that stops us seeing things as they are.

So his father and the uncle had succeeded after all. Theo became a (rather Greek) philosopher.

Common or Greek Tortoise: (*Testudo graeca*)

If Theo had seen the stone as it was seen by the tortoise who lived in its shade, he wouldn't have become a philosopher at all – or at least would have become a very different sort. To a creature that slow, the stone moved all the time. Its patina swirled, advanced, and retreated. The pace of the tortoise's world was the pace of its mind, which was the pace of its limbs. The boundary of last week's rain-stain rolled on to meet this week's boundary in what, to its basic brain, looked like an instant. In a world as exciting as a tortoise's, there was no time or mental space for a stone to be distilled or abstracted. There were no essences; only a pageant; a procession of fast evolving forms and stories. Tortoises live on a roller-coaster, or in the stalls of a theatre with a constantly changing programme.

And the tortoise (whose father knew Byron) wasn't tyrannised by sight. Sounds shuddered up its bones from the ground, bouncing off the inner surfaces as light zig-zags up a fibre-optic cable, making its face tremble and its chest thrum. Sounds and sights weren't related. They were separate performances in separate theatres. The tortoise's attention flicked between them, making notes in separate files.

The Author

It's not clear that the father and the uncle regarded Theo's philosophical career as a success. Since all Greeks were philosophers anyway, becoming a professional philosopher was hardly adding value. But it could have been worse, they agreed.

For Theo himself, though, perhaps it could not have been worse.

There were two possible directions for him. He might have said: 'The stone was material. Yet it was the gateway of the numinous.

Therefore matter matters.' He would have been helped in this by some of the more sophisticated neo-Platonists amongst the Greek Fathers.[18] That would have helped him to enjoy surf, steak, sex and flowers, and made him cherish the icon at the end of his bed.

But there was another road. This is the road he chose. It diverged at first only slightly from the first, but took him eventually in precisely the opposite direction. He started to see the stone as irrelevant compared to the abstraction to which it pointed. He started to denigrate matter. He got a hot lust for abstraction. He preferred the equation that described the arc of a swooping swallow to the swallow itself. He preferred the chemistry of taste to the taste itself. He loved generalities and feared specifics. He preferred the idea of a person to the person herself. He'd rather have a page from the letters of Abelard and Heloise than a midnight knock on his door.

He was, in other words, a miserable, proud, bloodless, sexless, friendless prig, perfectly suited for the top-down, Manichaestic world of professional philosophy.

It is terribly dangerous to be very good at something – particularly when the expertise is supposedly in the meaning of life and the fabric of thought. If you're told in your twenties that you're a master of those subjects, you're in deep trouble. Isn't it bound to arrest your development?

Theo

No. There were no tears in our house. What would have been the point? What had happened was too big and too dirty to be washed out by a bit of salt water.

Your talk about 'stone-ness' is adolescent earnestness of a kind I haven't heard for quite a while. Most of us flush that sort of debate out of the system in our late teens.

I was indeed fixated on a rock for a while, but that was the work of the beer I'd just had – my very first. If these sorts of Platonic epiphanies are caused by the light of Hellas, you'd expect Platonists to be commoner in, for instance, the east of England, where there's less moisture in the atmosphere, than in Wales or the Lake District. Are they?

Yes, I liked theory. I still do. Is there really anything very significant about that? Isn't it just an illustration of the general human desire to see the big picture?

You're right that the Greek trip left one mark. That mark, though, was the conviction that nothing – nothing - can hold out for long against kindness and dignity.

The wild kids! Pathological romanticism. Were they really ideal humans, uniquely connected to the world; perceiving things as they really are? Their noses ran, as I remember. Their knees were grazed; they wept and made bad decisions. If you must have idols, at least take note of their clumping clay feet.

Chorus

Well, we will see.

Time does not process, but unfolds, and when we look back we do not glance over our own shoulder only at our own footsteps in the sand, but we see places that were not uncovered when we walked through them

5. Philosopher

The Author

Theo's conspicuous ability to do what he was told took him to an old, smug, beautiful college in an old, smug, patchily beautiful university.

There he was described by all his tutors as 'brilliant', which, if the word connotes giving out light of one's own, was inaccurate. They meant that he was extremely good at reflecting what they beamed at him: of being like them. Since they considered themselves brilliant, that meant he must be brilliant too.

He spent three years writing model answers, sipping sherry, making complex plans to get into the knickers of a pale physicist from Thessaloniki called Elena, lying on a riverbank writing sonnets (because that was what one did), presenting papers of astonishing cleverness and superficiality to the Socratic Society, wandering in the vacations round the more obvious highlights of classical Greece, and sniffily cold-shouldering the wild kids (several of whom, somehow, had got to the university too, and were having a contemptibly good time in kayaks and jungles).

He was studying philosophy. The ancients thought that that was concerned to a large degree with how to live the good life. Theo, however, applied to work for a hedge fund – an occupation wholly inconsistent with every account of the good life ever articulated. He was saved by an administrative error.

By refusing to take seriously anything that the greats had said about how to be alive as a human, he got a spectacular degree. His father was pleased, and even smiled. There was a party in Theo's room, with vine leaves and meatballs, after which Elena finally capitulated. All fortresses had fallen. This, thought, Theo, was presumably what It Was All About. So why change it?

So he stayed. He learned quickly that original thoughts (at least since the end of the Hellenistic period) had been conceived only by shepherds, sailors and occasional journalists. Serious scholarship was appending footnotes to footnotes. Superb scholarship was appending footnotes to footnotes to footnotes. Not only was this easy: it was safe. And safety, if you'd come from northern Cyprus, wasn't to be sneezed at.

Yet the footnoting strategy made Theo uneasy. It was a Scholastic exercise: a Latin technique, from the wrong side of one of the great historical borders. He, despite everything, was Orthodox and Greek, marinated from conception in skepticism and faith: a faith dependent on skepticism; a skepticism made psychologically possible by faith. In the Academy there was a distinctively Western and distinctively mediaeval deference to the canonical authorities. You couldn't say that Hegel was wrong: you had to pussy-foot around him like an altar boy round an archbishop, suggesting that if he seemed absurd it was the reader's fault for not understanding him properly. Understanding would come by the multiplication of footnotes.

But that was the game, and games came easily to Theo. As part of the game, chortling at the deceit as he'd never laughed at anything as a child, he chose to write a thesis on one of the most revered philosophical saints: Kant. So for three lavishly funded years he seemed to genuflect and meekly swing the censer. In between services he learned the bouzouki and the tin whistle, baked bread, rode a motor bike increasingly fast around the Cotswolds, went to lectures about mountaineering expeditions which made him feel inadequate, charted the spread of mould across the ceiling of his Renaissance room, acquired successive passions for Dante, moths, Celtic saints, curry, cacti and rotifers, and never, ever, pretended to be interested in football.

His doctoral thesis might have had an Executive Summary that read: 'If Kant had had a good shag we'd all be a lot better off.' But so subtle were his ellipses that his examiners, after rising to applaud him at the end of the viva he had effortlessly controlled, went back to their rooms to pen a report of unprecedented sycophancy. 'The candidate has rewritten Kant scholarship. All subsequent scholars will have to take account of this work. We have been forced to revisit a number of our own conclusions – conclusions we thought unassailable.' Theo, running out of other sides of his face upon which to laugh, celebrated by eating sausage and chips from a roadside van near Cirencester.

ᚤᚤᚤ

Still more accolades followed. Glittering prizes hunt in packs. Theo dutifully packed them up and sent them back to Sheffield, and sometimes his father put on his funeral suit, came down to the college for a dinner, and sat at high table, bemused and satisfied, gravely answering questions from the well-mannered diners on either side; never venturing a question of his own, let alone a real view. At the end of the dinners a silver snuff box was passed round, and the bemusement and the satisfaction deepened. 'This is all I've done', said Theo to himself and to Elena. 'I've given him a silver snuff box, and it's enough; it's made up for everything. You're not a refugee if you've got a silver snuff box'.

But it wasn't enough. Every article had to be sent north: every conference invitation; every citation; every post card from an academic admirer. Quality or content didn't matter. The father couldn't judge them. It was all to do with philosophy, and thus assumed to be honourable. But since his father thought he was paid for his academic articles, quantity mattered, because even Aristotle had to pay his gas bills. The carefully catalogued files on the 'Theo' shelves back in the Sheffield bungalow swelled; the shelves bowed down towards the TV and the icons and the mother's photo.

Theo now had students of his own. He treated them with swash-buckling negligence - which meant that he coached them (and some-times couched them) brilliantly (that word again!) for their degrees - and they adored him. When one of them landed a plum job in the City, he'd raise an eyebrow, pour out some of his ritual madeira, congratulate them without any audible irony, and drink to their success.

Various Jurassic creatures

Theo isn't very likeable, but he can't be blamed. He lived in a college room built from Jurassic animals – from *us* - and so every square inch was a battlefield, and living in battlefields doesn't usually make people kind. Buried invisibly above his head as he slept was the tooth-marked tail-tip of an icythosaur. His coffee-machine leant against a crumbled clavicle of a crash-landed pterosaur. His books were dusty with the shells of bivalves that had surrendered to cephalopods – to belemnites, ammonites, and other squirting, squeezing, punching, sucking things. Or to hairy marine worms, whose shadows alone could be seen in the stone. Every glance at the wall was a frame from a geological snuff movie.

The stone still smelt of fear and strife. The electricity that had rip-pled along contending nerves still sat there, tight, blue and sibilant, coursing out into the air of tutorials and assignations. The belem-nites were batteries. They had not died. They had just been reorgan-ised and redistributed. They sputtered out into sherry, sentences and the edges of words; into the fingers and glances of undergraduates; into the flames that flowed up the chimney from the wood that itself was old, hard sunlight. Theo stared each night into those flames until he heard the porters open the gates to let out the early morning rowers.

If you live in a war, or watch snuff movies all day and night, it's bound to mark you.

The Author

In his long holidays, Theo went to Greece. 'I'm off', he told his colleagues, 'to my little Aegean hidey-hole.'

It was revealing language, for in most of Greece there is nowhere to hide. There is the stripped land, the sky, and the sea: always and everywhere the sea. And the Self: or sometimes the Self: it is far more mutable than the sea: far less consistently present.

The philosophy of Greece, which you might have thought was the main attraction for Theo, is the stuttering conversation between this evanescent Self and the effervescent sea. That conversation can only happen out in the open: not in any hidey-hole.

The template of all Greek philosophy is Pythagorean. A syllogism is true *because* it is beautiful. A proposition is accurate *because* it is elegant. $A^2 + B^2 = C^2$ because to be so is to be poised. The gradual approximation of a thing to its form in a life well lived is a procession towards completeness and loveliness. Intuition is more powerful than induction because it proceeds from the place from which all things proceed and to which all things return.

Theo understood none of this in his Aegean hidey-hole.

Greece is not all – or not obviously – poised. Wherever you go – even in the metro from Athens airport – any half sensitive person hears the screams of the creatures torn by the maenads.[19] If you think that's pretentious, I say that you're a newcomer, an eccentric, an outlier. Your version of reality is vanishingly recent. A flash in the pan. It's just arrived, and will soon be gone. The gods can bide their time.

Theo went back and back to Attica, the Peloponnese and the Cyclades, where it — whatever it is - all happened; idiotically happy just to be there, neither knowing nor seeking: as bovine as someone of his intellect can ever be. He was taut and predatory in a library; he was lowingly placid over the souvlaki. He didn't realize that the place was out to get him, to interrogate him, to make him give an account of himself; that every Greek word is a subpoena.

Greece could have unmade and re-made him. That it didn't means either that he was near divine or unusually shallow.

ΨΨΨ

One late September day he was on an island looking out towards Crete, listening to the heaving of the sea and sketching out a cunning little piece on Derrida, when the phone rang. It was an aunt. She was worried about his father. 'He's terribly weak', she said, 'and his breathing's very irregular. Please tell him to go to hospital. And please come home.'

She put his father on the line. 'I'm fine', he insisted. 'They're fussing. And of course you mustn't come back.'

ΨΨΨ

'The waters of death closed over the head of our beloved Yiorgios', intoned the priest. 'But he had passed already through the waters of baptism, and so was borne up onto the far bank.'

As a description of the mechanics of salvation, thought Theo, that was pretty unconvincing.

He was too furious to be sad. Furious at his father for not recognizing the approach of death, or, if he had, for lying about it. Furious at his father for dying when he did; dragging him back from the island just as something was about to happen; without having answered all the questions Theo had never put; without having become the sort of man he might have been. And furious at his father for dying at all. It was a contemptible abdication of the role of father, which entailed being alive. It had ushered in for Theo - and presumably for his father - a completely new mode of being. This had been done entirely without discussion, let alone with consent. It was underhand.

There had been no proper ceremony. On Tuesday night, shortly after the phone call, his father's soul had trickled out through the breeze blocks and the cavity insulation. It was casual, suburban and disrespectful: life and death were more serious than that; ask Tolstoy or Hardy. Since each person is an ecosystem, every death is ecocide. And it was vandalism: everyone is a library, and to die is to torch irreplaceable archives. It meant that Theo's past could no longer evolve. And it was, in the circumstances, particularly cruel. It meant a double bereavement for Theo. His father was the last link to his mother. The last bit of her died with him. What gave his father the right to kill his mother? That was a Turkish sort of thing to do.

It also posed an immediate, continuing, and very practical problem. Where should Theo send his prizes? If there was nowhere to send them, what was the point of getting them? That piece on Derrida, for instance. It was destined for a journal even his father would have known. His father would have read the abstract with admiring incomprehension, put it by his chair for a week or so, flicking occasionally through it during the nine o'clock news, and then filed it.

That was what it was there for: that was its only point. Only Theo knew how cynical and inconsequential it was. If there was no Theo-shelf in Sheffield, the article could not be justified.

That, for the moment, didn't stop him writing because writing was what he did and what he did was what he was and a death didn't stop him being what he was.

Theo started going up to the Sheffield house to write. For nearly half a century his father had used the house for sitcoms, early nights and dahlias. No one ever came, no one ever celebrated. Yet now the place was pregnant with him. And pregnancy means possible birth. Perhaps he'd never got past the cavity insulation after all. The father inhabited the house in death as he never had in life. He seemed desperate to be noticed just as, in life, he'd been desperate to be unnoticed. He was diligent and frenetic. Radios switched on. Lights switched off. His shirts smelt more of him the more they were washed.

Perhaps we all have a certain amount of living – inhabitation – to do, and those who don't use up their quota when they're alive do it when they're dead. It certainly seemed that way with Theo's dad.

Theo was interested and troubled. *What* had been left unlived? Was it being lived now? If so where and how? Could he join in?

Theo had waited until his father died before thinking he could un-derstand him. This was philosophically respectable and emotionally banal. Aristotle said that a life is only comprehensible when taken as a *whole*.[20] And so you can't start to assess it until it is ended. Theo had made a start on the Aristotelian audit of his father's life while waiting in Athens for the plane back to Heathrow. This strange busi-ness of the radios, the lights, and the shirts threatened to frustrate the audit.

In the little garden, beside the dahlias, was a bench where the father used to sit. On the morning of the death a neighbour had seen a carrion crow sitting there, its head leaning on the armrest. The crow was now there at eleven thirty each day – which just happened to be the time when the father's heart had finally given up. Theo looked at it. It looked mildly back. At about this time, Theo wrote in his notebook:

'1. Somewhere in the English Midlands a much-loved Master of Foxhounds was buried on a Friday. The meet was held as usual on the Saturday. The hounds found in the first covert. A big grey fox ran straight from there to the churchyard and over the Master's grave. Hounds lost him there.[21]

2. When a crew member died unexpectedly on board a boat, a dolphin was the first to notice the death.[22]

3. Elephants carry around the bones of dead elephants. They sometimes bury dead humans. They're not interested in the remains of any other species.[23]

4. Where effort is expended on making something, it's obvious that something of the maker inheres in the thing. No one would say that there is nothing of Leonardo in the Mona Lisa, but no one bothers to try to say what that something is. Perhaps when there has been insufficient effort, the effort that should have been expended continues to try to inhere somewhere. Perhaps there's a craving – or some sort of thermodynamic imperative - for incarnation. Perhaps all energy or (if it's different) personality, is looking for a home: a sink. Perhaps the sinks become <u>batteries</u>. Perhaps I could put wires on that standing stone at the top of the road and run a ceiling fan off it.'[24]

For a while after he made these notes Theo mooched round junk shops and derelict farms. He slept on the edge of the moor, under bracken in the woods, and, particularly, in the lee of dry stone walls.

He paced along the walls, noting the moods and ages of the wallers encoded in the strata; how a young and earnest man filled very care-fully, using bigger stones that his back could take; how the young man couldn't see the whole wall before it was built; how the older man knew that only impossible relationships would work. He cracked open a top stone, expecting a murmur of conversation, trapped since the nineteenth century, to trickle out. He saw the lines the walls habitually took; their preference for slight concavities; their suspicion of oblique climbs. The walls followed fossil forests; the law followed the walls; human longing and envy followed the law.

He began to see many other habits. A magpie woke at 4.50 a.m. and went to wash its beak in a pond. Light had a habit of travelling at 186,000 miles a second. The sun tended to rise in the east, and water ran obsessively downhill. Rabbits wore down paths across the grass.

He looked at a rabbit path. There had been a time before any rabbit foot had touched that ground. Then one rabbit came. It dashed from one clump of grass to another along the easiest and safest route. It did it again. Others joined it. The route became a track. Then walls went up, the clumps of grass vanished, and the geogra-phy of the valley changed so that the old path made no sense. Yet rabbits still went along it because they always had; it was part of their culture. The habits of live rabbits were determined by the habits of dead rabbits, which were determined by the habits of the valley. Why should his father's *komboloi* – in the habit of taking a particular path round his fingers – not continue to swing when the finger bones had pushed through the finger ends in a Yorkshire cemetery?

He saw that in the city, as everywhere, life had a habit of pushing out non-life. Groundsel split concrete blocks; lichens turned skimmed cement to landscape. Even in glass and steel malls, packs of Pucks leapt out, hooting and tooting, belabouring planners and architects with bladders; asserting ownership. For malls too, like our guts, hearts, lungs and brains, are wild places. It is laughable to think that we control them. A swab from the father's antiseptic kitchen would have grown an exuberant bacterial metropolis.

Unnerved, Theo went back to his own culture, which he'd been used to describing as 'high'.

As a requiem for his father, a friend had sent a link to a clip showing a beautiful woman playing a Mozart piano concerto. Theo watched it, horrified. The pianist lived in the music. There was nothing of herself outside it.

The clip was filmed in a stark, empty, but distinctly civilized human concert hall, but the film cut regularly to pictures of a winter wood. There was no dissonance between this human high culture and the wild. They expounded each other: there was no war against the wild. The pianist, just as she was in that concerto (Dior jacket and all) would have been as completely at home in the wood as a wolf.

ᚤᚤᚤ

Theo did what he always did when he didn't understand something: he wrote a really smart article about it. Then, badly shaken, he flew again to Greece.

He sat on a wooded hillside, looking out but seeing nothing but the terrible birdlessness of the Aegean — a birdlessness that asserts the supremacy and confidence of the sea. It needs (he thought) and will tolerate no supporting cast, let alone whirring, clattering things. It has no script: it just breathes. The habit of breathing crushes and forms rocks and civilizations, and grinds whale-ways deep into its own body.

The name of power, which makes and unmakes, is the Holy Name: the Tetragrammaton: *Yod, Heh, Vav, Heh.* Why those four consonants, asks David Abram?[25] Because, he says, they are the consonants that sound most like vowels – which are unwritten in Biblical Hebrew. And why *this* combination of vowels? Because they are the vowels that sound most like the breath: the holy tide. You need to breathe in order to *be.* When God is asked who he is, he replies (as the priest had told Theo all those years ago): 'I am who I am', which might be paraphrased as: 'I am the ground of being: I *am being.*' If you're aware of breathing (which can be achieved with a lot of practice) you know that you *are* and *you* are. What was it that hovered over the face of the pre-existent deep? The holy breath. It's still hovering, thought Theo: listen! It's the Tetragrammaton that sweeps across the bay and fills the sails and makes the water old and new.

It would be neat if, at this point, Theo had slapped his forehead, shouted 'Of course!', stood up on the shingle, nodded gratefully to the sea and marched off to begin a new life of humbled enlightenment. But he didn't. He did indeed get up and march off, but it was to a taverna owned by a local showman known for lifting up tables with his teeth. There he drank a bottle or two of wine before walking into town to seek refuge from metaphysics between the legs of a Swedish nurse he'd met the previous week.

ᚤᚤᚤ

He woke suddenly. It was still dark. He was sweating into her. Owen Barfield, he recollected as the nurse snored, had been lunching in C. S. Lewis's rooms in Oxford. Lewis, who was then a philosophy tutor, referred to philosophy as a 'subject'. 'It wasn't a subject to Plato', said Barfield. 'It was a way.'[26]

Theo caught the next flight to England. He had made a start.

ΨΨΨ

For a while nothing much seemed to have happened.

As a patriotic Greek philosopher, Theo continued to teach the joys and benefits of the *polis* until the memory of the moor, the fields, the woods and the sea had retreated into a deep stratum of his mind, only occasionally exposed by an eruption of sudden wildness: a swift on the end of a scream, or the clash of clouds.

As his father had done before him, he recruited allies to keep the wildness out: formal clothes, neat systems of ideas, tidy Baroque music; and, most promisingly, alternating secularism and geometric Protestantism, both of which tried to keep the raging gods of wind and blood penned behind hedges of propositions.

But he knew he was under siege. Even some of those allies began to look dodgy.

ΨΨΨ

He might have mitigated his fear by buying into the wilderness industry: protecting himself from a nasty infection of virulent wildness by submitting to a small injection of attenuated wildness. By subscribing to some sort of actual or metaphorical magazine that served up nature-lite, perhaps: the birds always broadside on for easy recognition; no punctured viscera; no leeches dangling from ducks' nostrils. But he had a disdain for clubs – even those clubs characterized not by formal membership but by a shared taste for zipped fleece jackets, or the badge of a type of binoculars, or the jaunty swing of a spotting scope.

He had a patrician dislike of breathable clothing and unnecessary layers and, more reasonably, contempt for the twitcher's ruling axiom: the heresy, trashed by Darwin a hundred and fifty years ago, that species are immutable.

'Why peer so earnestly down your scope?', he'd ask. 'Or rummage through your field guide in search of an eye-stripe or a tail bar? What you've ticked off in your little black book doesn't really exist. It didn't exist, even in your terms, a million years ago, and it won't exist, even for you, in another million years. It isn't 'it' at all. It's part of a process. To name it is like naming the particular motion of one tooth at one time in one cog. And if you don't get that', said Theo, 'you don't understand time; and if you don't understand time, you don't understand nature, because nature is just what time does with a load of molecules. So you'll never get me on one of your air-conditioned buses to a promising swamp.'

Argument, for Theo, had always been a way of avoiding real engagement. Now, to the surprise and amusement of his colleagues, he argued constantly and passionately about the place of humans in the natural world.

Those gentle, list-ticking twitchers, he insisted, were part of a Nietzschean drive to mastery, living out, in their hides and their Goretex the disastrous (or at least disastrously misunderstood) command to subdue the earth.[27] Every tick was an assertion of dominion over the birds of the air. Birdwatching was a sort of farming: information farming. It was all about erecting fences round the wild places for the purpose of control, and ultimately of self-aggrandisment.

'That seems a bit *harsh*', protested a mild Classicist whose son had just joined the school bird-watching club.

'Harsh?' said Theo. 'Not at all. They want to be Kings. They've got to be stopped. I'd string 'em up on gibbets at the gates of nature reserves, *pour encourager les autres.*'

'Bird*watching?*', he'd say. 'Bird*watching* is almost unknown. Your son's turning into a bird *spotter*. There are plenty of them, and they're vermin. Bird *watching* is redemptive, because if you watch birds you'll eventually know that you're watched *by* birds, which will put you properly in your place.'

Then, warming to his theme, and pouring out another glass of red wine, he'd be off, denouncing the notion of measurement, and soon, convinced by his own voice, he was sure he was right to stay indoors, by the gas fire in his college room, rather than have the purity of his notions about the wild compromised or contradicted by a real beak or tail or mud bank.

In his better moments (between glasses five and six) he knew that he wouldn't go to the wild because it would find him out, as its worms eventually find us all out. 'Who are you?', it would ask, and 'Theo', he would say, and 'Liar!' it would bellow or breathe back. Greece had taught him that there was nowhere to hide *out there*. From which he had concluded, illogically, that there might be somewhere to hide *in here*. So, between glasses seven and eight he'd tell himself that his debt to authenticity was best paid by elegant articles on identity and personhood. The reviewers might sometimes bite, but not as badly as a wolf.

ᛉᛉᛉ

It couldn't last. The ontological vertigo finally got to him. Queasy for a year or so, he woke one morning to find that a decision had been made. He was never clear by *whom*.

It was a decision, in the first instance, to refuse to play the academic game. 'Humans stride', he declaimed, leaping out of bed. 'They don't slither.'

He yawned, farted, and ate all the cake at Faculty meetings. He made laconic observations at seminars, along the lines of: 'Bollocks'. He wrote nothing for a couple of years. He began to teach his students what he'd learned, and when they failed their exams he cheered. Pressed by the Head of Department to justify his existence by applying for a grant, he wrote on the application to an august benevolent organization (in 12 point Times New Roman, as prescribed by the rubric): 'I would like lots of money, please, to continue (on high and ancient Athenian authority) being a gadfly biting the pale and flabby arse of the intellectual Establishment.'

In a truly civilized society this would have produced a huge cheque and immediate promotion. Instead it produced a summons to attend a disciplinary tribunal.

Theo replied, inviting the tribunal to meet him, at the hour appointed for the hearing, at a local pub. 'The drinks are on me', he wrote. 'But I'll be on the hemlock.'

He was dismissed by an unpunctuated text message.

ᚹᚹᚹ

He returned to his college. He wrote a short note to the Master, thanking him for the good times, surrendering his room, and apologizing for all the bother, and another, to a colleague with whom he'd sometimes read Norse sagas and drunk mead, asking her to take whatever was left in his rooms to a charity shop. 'Except Kant', he added. 'Burn him'.

Into the sidecar of his old motorbike he piled an unlicensed shotgun, a waterproof sleeping bag, a knife used by his grandfather to disembowel a janissary, 'The Boys' Book of Tracking', a manual of maritime navigation, some old-fashioned oilskins he'd found in a skip in Piraeus, a fishing line, cooking gear, a diving mask and snorkel, a Greek New Testament, lots of his father's old clothes, a set of *komboloi* from Nafplio, photos of his parents, the key texts from Mircea Eliade and Joseph Campbell,[28] the *Morte d'Arthur,* some of the great Greek classics of prose and poetry, both ancient and modern, a tin whistle, lots of baked beans and pot noodles, some very valuable wine, his old notebooks, and a seal skull. He slung his bouzouki on his back.

He went southwest because he'd have the wind at his back.

Theo

Oh dear, oh dear, oh dear. My fears are being realized. We've got all the ingredients of recipe-book Greek fantasy: dark gods, olive grove epiphany, thyme-scented air, a whispering (no, sorry, *breathing*) sea, a crude animism which allows a lazy writer to personalize the land-scape without working to sketch the personality accurately, and even a bit of sex.

While we're on the sex, what does it mean to 'seek refuge from meta-physics' between someone's legs? Nothing, so far as I can see. Vac-uous over-writing which might sound clever until you give it a moment's thought.

It's true that I reflected on habits, but instead of embracing some sort of pop pan-psychism, I noted that most morality is habitual, and started to believe (hardly an original conclusion) that you could derive moral precepts from the habitual alignment of the universe. There is, in other words, no 'is-ought' gap:[29] there's nothing disrep-utable about concluding what you should do from the way the world is - or if there is a gap it's not as yawning or dangerous as it's made out to be. Isn't that more interesting and significant than occult spec-ulations about the perpetual motion of my dead father's worry-beads? Why should the beads not continue to swing? *Because my father is bloody dead,* that's why. Science may not be my strong suit, but even I know that dead fingers don't move.

And a warning: leave my father alone. No grief can be shared, say the agony aunts. That's because no grief can be described. That's because no person can be described. How dare you.

Understand, please, that there is no comfort in your mystically circular view of life. It doesn't help, whatever dreadlocked, unwashed people say, to hear that my father has been recycled. It diminishes him and you. His trajectory was linear, and if he's still got a trajectory, it still is. He started at one point, and ended at quite another. The distance between those points was his story. You need to be a story to be significant, and there are no circular stories – or if there are, they are far, far more boring than any human who has ever lived. Though his molecules may have become part of an ocelot or a cheese pie, he hasn't. He isn't his molecules, you reductionist retard. There's no sense whatever in which *he* will be *again*. He either persists, if those sinister black-hatted priests are right, or he doesn't.

You overstate the drama of my intellectual development. I just got older, and so began to know what changes people, and the pace of that change. Ideas other than moral ideas aren't terribly important, and even when they do cause change, they don't do it in Eureka moments. There are no philosophical messiahs outside psychiatric hospitals.

You overdramatize, too, my interest in the natural world. If you must know, I rather fancied a woman who was doing a PhD on geese. I learned twitcher-language so I could stalk her, and then found that my digestion was better if I took the odd country walk.

Most offensive, though, is the insinuation that I'm newly in thrall to some atavism that has come oozing out of Hallam Moors, or the Parthenon, or the corpse of some ancestor. That I've gone over to the wild side. That I've renounced form so that I can worship some amorphous force – but a force, incoherently, with horns, hoofs and pipes.

To be clear: No system without form, and therefore restraint, is truly wild or, therefore, truly exciting. An example: There's nothing remotely erotic about the thrashings or gyrations of a nightclub. Anyone with normal libido knows that it flourishes best within the elaborate turns of a quadrille; that the touch of a shoulder tip as the lines of dancers pass is far more steamily tumescent than hips grinding into each other.

But I'm glad that the myth of my departure from academia is evolving so colourfully.

I daresay you'll give yourself the final word. That's pretty shabby, you know.

The Author

Humans rarely think that they are as exciting or as complex as they really are. Theo is no exception.

He's right: I should have said more about the moral effects of his journey. Perhaps I need only add that, after his father's death, he refused to write about the things that he knew would be best for his career: Kant, Hegel, Schopenhauer. This was because he couldn't stomach their company. 'Imagine writing a biography of Eichmann', he'd say. 'You'd get up each morning, have your toast and marmalade, and then spend the day in the company of a psychopath, with pee breaks. Who'd do that?'

Perhaps that was progress. Or perhaps he was beginning to think that Kant, Hegel, and Schopenhauer were Turks.

I should also have said that for about three hours a day, and five at weekends, he wept out of pity for things; and particularly for the things that never were. For hatching mayflies eaten by trout; for his mother's old age; for potted caviar; for the shed at the bottom of his parents' garden where he'd never hosted the Wild Kids and never stuffed squirrels; for the Second Coming, and for someone to tell him he was stupid.

<u>Chorus</u>

It is something and not nothing to start, but not all ends are there in the beginning.

Only the gods see all, and then only all the gods together, in conclave on the mountain. One goddess by herself, because of her too-great love for a mortal, may be blind.

<u>Theo</u>

Oh, do be quiet. Bloody sanctimonious, portentous Greeks.

6. To the little brown sea

The Author

At Bristol the wind changed, and he needed another reason to go in a particular direction. Failing to find one, he was free, for the first time in four decades, of any reason at all.

He sped south-westwards with a powerful conviction: the sort of conviction, he supposed, that fuelled Mississippi creationists and migrating wildebeest.

It was dark, and starting to rain, when his front wheel went into a hole in a small steep road, and he went head first into a hedge. He took that as a sign. Of what, he wasn't sure, and it didn't bother him. Most of us never ask what our signs signify.

He pushed the bike through a farm gate, let it fall behind a pile of hay bales, decanted the sidecar into a couple of rucksacks and followed the hedge downhill. A cloud burst over his head and his clothes and hair fizzed with ions that a fortnight before had been above a kittiwake colony in Newfoundland.

He pushed on into a wood. It felt tired. The canopy was thick and the floor was dry. He pulled out his sleeping bag, cushioned his head on the bouzouki, and went to sleep staring into the empty orbits of the seal skull.

Carrion crow

A crow sitting on an oak branch in the wood absorbed all the wavelengths of light that seeped through the leaves in the early morning.

She reflected none, and if Theo had seen her he would have said she was black. It just meant that she was greedier for colour than non-black things.

Theo, had he seen her, would have said too that she was looking at him. But it is not clear what this could have meant. It is not clear what the 'she' was.

The data streaming in through Theo's right eye passed, via the optic nerve, to both the right and left sides of his brain. The whole of his brain processed the right-sided information and integrated it with the information coming from the left eye to form a picture of the world to which both eyes had contributed. Theo could coherently say: 'This is *my* view of the world.' But the crow could not. The left side of her brain didn't talk to her right. There was no conversation along the lines of:

Left side: *'That dead rabbit looks good. I'm going to get it.'*
Right side: *'I wouldn't if I were you: there's a fox crouching behind the tree.'*
Left side: *'Thanks for the warning. I'll leave it for the moment.'*

Inside the crow's head there were two distinct worlds: the world of the right and the world of the left. You could teach her left side one trick, while leaving the right completely ignorant. Imagine your left side reading *Hamlet* and your right side watching *Mamma Mia*. The crow's life was like that.

Yet wasn't there some central 'I'? Wasn't it the 'I' - not the right or the left side - that was interested in not being eaten by a fox? Is it hopelessly misconceived to say to a schizophrenic on a bridge: 'Hello, John: please don't jump'? - using the name on his birth certificate rather than addressing all his parts?

Theo, for the moment, was in the world of the crow's right brain, and played a major part in it. The right side of the crow (and the left one, for that matter) had only ever seen an immobile human once before, when a child in a plastic dinghy drifted out towards Wales and was swamped. The child had floated in a couple of weeks later, peeled, with bladder wrack for hair. The right side of the crow had found this interesting. So both sides were particularly interested in this other immobile human that seemed to have the same sort of hair as mobile humans.

The right side watched Theo for a while. Then, unnerved, it sought corroboration from the left, and caused the head (which it shared with the left side) to move – suggesting that the right side knew of the existence of the left, even if it didn't know much about the content of the left's world. The left and the right agreed that, unlike the child, this didn't seem edible.

If we can talk meaningfully about *a* bird, this bird flew off from a beech branch to an oak top. *She* flew exactly along the border between the two unconnected universes of her two sides. *She* was in the no-man's land between them. If anything at all could connect the two universes, it was the mysterious *she*. But the problem with that sort of suggestion was that the *she* was *herself* partly a creature of each of the universes.

Whatever *she* was, and wherever *she* was, *she* was hungry. The glandular stomach and the gizzard, which processed mice, eggs, and slugs from both the left and right worlds, were shared by the right and left brain. The gizzard ground for both and each. And so this notional bird, from the top mast of the swaying oak, saw a seal pup on the tide line just below the wood, and flapped down onto it.

The Author

Theo was woken by what he thought was a breath. Then there was a true breath – the gasp of a tree – and he knew his anatomy was wrong. He'd heard a gut.

The ruling marine metaphor is the maw. Sea noises are all alimentary. The sea gurgles and sometimes slaps its belly. Its main movement is peristalsis. It wants to eat you. When it does, all it'll give back is a belch that will smell briefly of you before it's wafted into a guillemot's air sacs to become the latest squawk.

Theo stood up and rubbed his eyes. The wood was on a finger of rock pushing out into an angry brown sea – angry with the finger, angry with Theo, angry with the mess of earth and leaves that spilled into it, angry with the presumption of the land, angry and very, very old. It had chewed away at England, but England wasn't going quietly. The land defiantly sprouted, flowered and hummed.

Over to the north was a long flat stone beach, covered in weed. Behind and beyond was a small grey town. The beach was as pristine as an operating theatre. Every bit of plastic was ground and every stone scrubbed, as if the sea wanted to make a show of its hygienic – and thus moral – superiority to the shitty alleys running next to the shore.

The tide was out. When it came in, the weed would rise and dance on the feet that tethered it to the rock.

The wave Theo now watched had been calved somewhere near Barbados, as slices of water were slashed from an underwater face.

The slices had slid forward, fallen for a moment, and reared up into the hot wind. They processed sedately across the Atlantic, bounced off a Mauritanian sand bank, collided with another phalanx of slices that had started life near Greenland, spun north-east, collected themselves again, punched into a Portuguese beach where a couple were having adulterous sex at midnight, drove into Biscay, caught up a raft of plastic bags, condoms, and fish heads which they dumped at Land's End, and pushed on past Devon, growling at the pasty and pixie shops. As they saw the town, they reassembled into one block of water which swung up as it had when young - but getting this time a white foam crown - and curled round into itself with a terminal crash.

Theo saw only a wave, and a party of Belz Hasidim from Stamford Hill picking ornithologically through the rock pools, *peyos* swinging like turkey wattles.

Theo pulled out his binoculars and followed them. Prayer time came, and they stood on stones, feet tightly together, and bobbed. Theo wondered if they were thanking Yahweh for caging Leviathan with the cliffs, and whether there was a Yiddish word for 'anemone', coined in a Lithuanian *shtetl* to illuminate a Talmudic allusion.

The prayers done, they snapped their prayer books shut, piled into a row of enormous minibuses and sped off to eat, while they blinked at a patch of howling moor, food endorsed by a rabbi in Golders Green.

Theo put down his binoculars. He just sat. That was new for him. He felt grass under him. That was new too. He noticed that he was breathing and assumed that he had been breathing up until then. The oxygen – some of which dissolved in his blood and pumped round his brain, helping to make the next thought – had been used by dragons, Vikings, camp fires, albatrosses, and actuaries.

He saw the gulls that stood on the sand where a river brought farmland in solution to the sea. There were drowned land snails here, their extruded bodies improbably long, grown fat on grass sprung from red deer dung.

It took a lot to make these gulls move. They too just sat or stood. They brought mess to that clinical beach: vomit, moult and slime. Gull mess has the feel of a pubertal bedroom.

The eyes of gulls are the coldest things. Compassion must have evolved after they did. All birds are modified dinosaurs: gulls are unmodified dinosaurs. The coldness concentrates with each generation.

Their cruelty is more obscene because they are so tidy, neat, systematic, and economic. Their heads are never spattered with entrails, bile or blood; never ruffled. Even when they draw blood from each other, it spreads tastefully over the white neck, as claret on linen. They're freshly starched nurses. Their beaks stab methodically like demonic sewing machines.

They turn Manx Shearwaters neatly inside out. It's one thing to be laid flat, eviscerated, and picked clean. It is quite another to be turned inside out like a sock. It's more barbarous to be killed neatly than in a frenzy of pecks and rips. Gulls don't have the decency to be frenzied. The death of any creature mandates an oblation of excitement; warrants mess and frenzy; some sort of sign that it's not the norm. It's the control that's scary. You can argue with a glutton: never with a nurse.

That gulls should be white – and *so* white – should make you question the bona fides of the universe.

Theo thought none of these things. He thought nothing. The pain, the problems and the joy of the beach were merely there. At mid-afternoon, hunger was merely there; a fact relating to his stomach, which itself was simply where it was, just as the limpets were on the rocks and the crow was on the tree behind him. They could be where they were, and the way they were, without being discussed.

When he was drenched by rain he noted that he was wet, as one might note the passage of a distant cloud.

Carrion crow

Both halves and the whole of the crow knew that this thing on the beach was the same thing that had moved that morning, and that it was the sort of thing that could be dangerous. They knew that it did not have a gun – the usual means by which such things killed – and on their two wings and two legs they came confidently closer than a shotgun's range to investigate. They saw a moving chest and blinking eyes. This, they concluded, meant that the thing was likely to persist for a while, and be dangerous for a while, before it became food.

There was more to the thing than food and danger. The whole of the crow, and possibly each half, liked to be entertained. Novelty was itself a kind of entertainment. The thing was new to the beach, and behaving in an odd way for a biped, and therefore on balance, and despite its dangerousness, was to be welcomed and protected. So when a gull, without any of this meticulous reflection, landed next to Theo with a view to eating his tongue, the crow landed on the gull's neck and took out his right eye.

Herring gull

This conferred on the gull a new and puzzling sort of integration. It now lived purely in the left world. The crow cured the gull of his schizophrenia; of the tense non-discourse of his hemispheres. The gull was in his right (by which the author means left) mind.

The Author

In later life, when the law practice or the business can manage without them, the wife can be provided for, and the children have flown the nest, Brahmins traditionally prepare for the transmigration of their souls by walking into the forest, seeking privation and enlightenment.

This was not what Theo had done. He was running from death, not towards it. And he didn't go to the wild: the wild came to get him.

ΨΨΨ

When the dark slunk out of the sea and up the beach that first night, Theo went with it, back into the wood.

Through the night, sweating, grunting, urgently, he dug a hole under an old beech tree, pulling out stones, cracking the earth along old fault lines, and scrabbling with his hands until his nails split and his fingers bled.

The moon climbed, shining the cold light of the gull's one eye onto his back. By midnight he could get his head and shoulders underground. By dawn he had a home the size and shape of a sleeping bag. He wriggled inside, and with his head on a moss pillow slept until the sea again swallowed the sun. The earth writhed round him like a uterus trying to push him out. He breathed in his sleep to the metronome of the waves. Then he got up, pissed, shat, wiped himself on leaves, ate some beans, shat again, pushed his way through the blackberries, undressed, and walked towards the sea.

It's not clear why. There's a strong temptation to get all symbolical, and there's too much of that in this book. Perhaps it was just because he smelt bad and was sticky with soil.

The moon was behind cloud. There was fog in Wales, and only a faint hum of light came across the water from the steel-works and housing estates. The street lamps of the little grey town threw orange bars onto the sea: black, orange, black, orange. The sea was like a tiger or a wasp.

Things sighed under his feet. A hard wind blew full in his face. Sand rasped him. His nose was etched by a sand-grain shaped by a glacial wind several ice ages ago.

The sea creaked and fizzed. He walked into it.

ᚤᚤᚤ

He couldn't see it coming. Not even when it pulled itself up with a groan and slumped on top of him. It gathered him; tucked him in; took him out and down and in. There there was no direction; no gravity; just the buzz of repatriated particles of land slipping over each other. There was no timeline – there were no lines at all - and so no anticipation. The sea was more full of things than his own body was full of components, and so he couldn't diffuse into it, and so dissolution wasn't possible, and so neither was fear. It was merely a fact that he was here, and that fact was interesting. He was spun as he hadn't been since he was in the hands of a gruff Cypriote obstetrician, but this spin was aimed at getting him into a huge amniotic sac rather than out of a little one.

He went down, or possibly up, or possibly sideways, and his head hit something hard. That too was merely interesting. It wouldn't have been seemly to gasp, and so he simply noticed that there wasn't much breath in his chest, and that he'd soon have to breathe water instead. It seemed fair enough. Why not?

Cold bodies bumped him. Something slithered under his armpit. The sea hissed and smelt blue. Crack: Hiss: Crack: Hiss.

There were other sounds now. Always a conversation; lilting, lisping. Sometimes a choke, a gag, a hoick. The sea was bringing him up or failing to get him down. He hit his head again. A rock gently, expertly and surgically laid open his leg from ankle to knee. The proportions of sodium in his blood and in the seawater were almost identical, and so it didn't matter much. He opened his eyes and shut them again fast because the beauty was too much.

The beauty saved him. Not only was it a category, where there had been no categories before, but it was a desirable category, where there had been no desire before.

Suddenly he wanted brown bread, a lamb chop, and a string quartet – preferably all at the same time.

Time! Time was suddenly back, along with other conventional dimensions. Up was up and down was down, and he was going down and he shouldn't be, and there was the splendour of pain and fear.

For some reason or none the sea relented. It breathed him out. His head broke the surface and air flooded into him, meeting seawater on the way out. There was a queasy, inconclusive contest for jurisdiction.

ΨΨΨ

He was miles out and bleeding. The cloud had cleared. He could see stars and, on the Welsh side, occasional vehicles on the coast road.

He remembered how comfortable he'd been as a child, lying awake in his grandparents' home in Nicosia next to a busy road: kept awake by the companionable rumble that meant he was sharing the night with someone else. The Welsh lorries weren't companions. Their lights taunted him. They might as well have been on the moon. They were the lights of vehicles driven by people who would know what tomorrow was like. Theo was now interested in tomorrow, and felt cheated.

He was in the middle of the channel, and moving fast. A current six feet below the surface moved even faster and sloped down. If he let his legs fall, they were grabbed. He kicked free and lay on his back, circling towards Land's End. Surf from an underwater wave broke beneath him and shuddered through him.

He circled faster and faster. The stars grew tails. The sea around him was taut, then slack, then taut again, but not with the wind. He span faster, his arms outstretched, clutching to stop himself falling. His fists closed on spume.

A whiteness came out of the dark above and jolted away with a shriek as if it had seen a plague cross painted on the water. The circles got smaller. He started to spin around his own navel. Then the sea started to snore.

'Plug hole', thought Theo. 'Plug hole'.

Then there is a blank in his memory. Perhaps he lost consciousness. Perhaps he was too conscious for memories to implant. Perhaps there was just too much sensation for a re-tellable story to be told, or to be filed in a carefully curated brain.

ΨΨΨ

There was a thump in his ribs, too hard to be his heart. Something smooth slicked against him. Another thump turned him onto his side. The thump became a nudge, and the nudge became a push. There was a hot halitotic snort in his face. The push became a journey.

There was no more snoring. There were beech leaves in the water, and the sigh of waves hitting sand, and he was spat onto the beach he'd left. Behind him in the water a thwack, a flutter, and then nothing.

Dolphin

Exhausted by an afternoon of play with a gannet's wing and a strenuous evening's masturbation against a silkily weed-covered buoy, the dolphin was asleep, rolling gently on the surface. Or half of him was asleep. His breathing, unlike ours, was not automatic. If his brain didn't constantly tell his diaphragm to keep breathing, he would suffocate. So his right and left brain took turns napping. When the right brain was asleep, the right eye (oddly) was open, funneling information into idling neurones, and the left eye (strangely) was shut - which didn't help to keep the left brain awake and on the respiratory job.[30]

He was woken by the knowledge of something big and despairing. Though he could detect moods and truthfulness ultrasonically (different moods bounced ultrasound back with differing speeds, and dishonesty had a specific ultrasonic taste),[31] this had nothing to do with imaging. The water tingled, as the air stops tingling when someone dies. By an effort of will his left brain told his right brain to jump to it, and the right brain grumblingly complied.

What the whole animal then knew was that a nearby human was sad.

He had met humans before. They were usually in the ceiling, and loud, with a whirring blade below them that could take off a fin. Sometimes they were black, with long feet and humped backs. Then they breathed underwater, but the breathing was rasping and sick. It was hard to understand how they could stand on land with backs like that, or walk with feet like that. These humpbacked humans weren't sad, though their behaviour was often bizarre in a way seen only in very ill dolphins - like grabbing a fish and then releasing it.

This one lay on its back as if it were dead. But it was clearly not. The dolphin saw its ventricles spitting blood into tubes, the eddies round the valves, the air bags filling and emptying as a hooped wall of muscle pushed up against them and fell back. He saw the remnants of its last meal being squeezed round a roller-coaster of soft pipes and squirting out between its legs; and, almost, the thoughts bouncing round its head with the blood: a rush of blood to the outer layer of the brain as the human tried to reason a way back to the shore; a gush to an old, deep brain region, shared with the fish, as it smelt hope in a schooner's effluent.

Everything was transparent to the dolphin. There were no surfaces in his world – just boundaries between areas which dealt differently with his streams of screeching noise. He saw tapeworms bathing in the gut-soup of whales, the feathery gills of cod, neurological storms gusting in the north-east of a porpoise's head, and a Turkish bullet, c 1974, eroding Theo's aorta.

Cetaceans see us better than we see ourselves.

Like every creature, this dolphin knew about causation. He knew that if he closed his jaws around a salmon the salmon would stop behaving like a live salmon, and that this was *because* he had closed its jaws. He knew that if he closed his jaws and swallowed, hunger would go away. He knew that if the bullet moved a little further, blood from the big tube would fill Theo's chest.

The dolphin saw the bullet (a buckled squab of lead, half an inch long) from fifty yards away. Around it was a coagulated plug of the eastern Mediterranean. He knew that he would not like to have this in him. He knew that the man was not meant to be in the middle of the channel, but instead on the hard. The dolphin was a conservative creature, with a sense that things had their own places, and that it was usually better for them to stay there; indeed that the whole world was generally better if things kept to their places.

He pitied, so he pushed, nosing the man through the waves and shoving him onto the beach.[32]

The Author

On any decent view, Theo was now entitled to a break from *events*. And precisely because of this moral entitlement, he assumed that that's precisely what he wouldn't get.

He was wrong. In the language he now rightly distrusted, he was allowed for a while to *be* rather than *do*.

He washed out his leg wound with a bottle of burgundy from the college cellar, drank another bottle while stitching the leg with a sewing kit from a chain hotel, and slept dreamlessly, inhaling soil.

He was proud when he woke, because though the swallows and martins were going, he was staying, along with the trees, the limpets and the oystercatchers. Like the trees he was buried in the ground; like the limpets he was attached to a small bit of rock; like the oyster-catchers he'd continue to pipe away through the cold – though his tunes, on his tin whistle, were from Crete, Kerry and Benbecula. Like all of them he was dying (he could see it in the broken veins of his feet) but, like most of them, he would be around for a while.

In the meantime it was splendid. Beetles crawled over his boots. A tide of salt air flowed in and out of him. The crow looked at him with one side and then another. The summer sunlight was disguised as sugar and lay coiled in berries, ready to spring out in him and be turned again into light, heat and thought.

The wood and the sea were frantic with the knowledge of the approaching cold.

There were more fish than there had been for a year. The summer hung on, sequestered in fat; shiny, chubby, and sleek. The water was sticky with chlorophyll, throbbing with tiny cellular engines.

Young lampreys, spawned and raised in fresh moor and field water, came down to the sea, swimming with a terrible languid economy. When they tasted salt water for the first time they were suddenly savage. Their mouths ground through the bellies of salmon, cod and haddock. They clung on until the host died, sucked dry. They were a second body for the host while the host survived, and an immediate and literal reincarnation for it when it was dead.

The land swelled for a moment.

Though it was cooler than the summer, the surviving butterflies, defying their metabolism, flew faster and more desperately. At night the moths, blundering with old age and chill, flew hard into Theo's face as he sat against his beech tree, dusting his beard with silver scales. Leaves sprouted even as they yellowed. Bees gathered pollen for a spring they would never know.

Soon the surface water would cool and sink. The fish would sink with it. But sometimes a wedge of cool water would prise up a chunk of warmer sea, and for a few days, until wind and osmosis got to it, there would be a little island of summer in the middle of a winter sea.

New birds arrived. Dunlin brought lumps of arctic stone in their gizzards. Rafts of widgeon, hoping for a kinder winter than they'd get in Russia, swung round offshore, waiting for the falling tide to expose gutweed and sea lettuce. Sanderling, which a fortnight before had probed the paw-prints of Spitsbergen polar bears for crustaceans, scampered on the surf edge like voles on speed and stilts, spearing sewage in confusion.

Earthworms dragged into their burrows salt-sprayed leaves that had farmed light since April and lived through great storms. Salt shrivels worm guts. Stately slugs glided over the last of the dock leaves. The blackbirds (which knew now not to clink out an alarm when Theo walked through the wood) had beautiful purple dung from the blackberries. As the land exhaled, its breath now turned white.

No one came to the wood or to Theo's end of the beach. The fat town dogs and their panting owners were tired long before they came near him. The nearby fields had been fallow for years. There were occasional uninterested boats.

The main traffic was in the sky: purposeful birds, eyes and course set, with thoughts, plain as could be, of where they were going and what they would do there. These were thoughts of the future: abstractions of the same type as Theo's professional musings in the philosophy journals. The birds were imagining themselves (and therefore obviously knew what them*selves* were: knew *who* they were) eating lugworms and sandhoppers in an entirely theoretical future on a little island a couple of miles away. Their mental pictures of what that island was like now, and why it was worth all the effort, were collages of previous experiences, stuck together with memory, preference, bias and hope. If a peregrine came near, their fear of the annihilation of them*selves* pushed the island from their minds for a while.

Theo laughed in joy and despair. Joy because they were just like him, and he wasn't alone. Despair because they were just like him, and so he couldn't look to them for any sort of rescue.

He panicked. 'Facts' said Theo, aloud to the crow. 'I need facts'. The crow agreed. She was big on facts.

ΨΨΨ

The first thing it seemed important to know was just how change-able the apparently immutable things were. So, with a can of paint he found in a ditch, Theo painted the cliffs to see how fast they eroded (about a foot that winter), the limpets to see how far they wandered from their established homes (about a foot a day, grazing on local algae, and then back, before the challenge of the big surf, to their own bespoke depression),[33] and the backs of the beetles (to convince himself that there was a stable community around him).

Detail mattered as it never had before. He looked for scars, missing feathers, tics, habits, friendships, alliances and expression. Did that robin emphasise its final syllable? Didn't that raven's croak seem start unusually high in the throat? That old haddock grubbed just like a truffle-rooting pig.

That final form of comparison – the simile – depressed him. It seemed inescapable, but it was inescapably wrong. Nothing was like anything else.

'What vanity', the crow seemed to respond. 'You're just like every-one. You have no face. Nothing has. Live with it.'

Theo looked in a pool of water, and the wind blew across the water, and it was true: he had no face at all.

This was a very ancient state of affairs. Perversely it made Theo feel authentic.

First there were no faces. Look in any decent museum. Then there were faces with only eyes. The eyes said nothing. Noses were added in the Neolithic – noses unanatomically continuous with the forehead. Then, along with writing, some time in the Bronze Age, came anatomically accurate faces. But then, and for centuries afterwards, the faces were dull: they signified nothing.[34] In Periclean Athens the gods and heroes stared blankly out at the sea. There was nothing behind the eyes. They were magnificent mannikins. You'd never want to have dinner with them. They'd have no conversation. Nothing had ever happened to them, and nothing ever would. They were merely beautiful, and their beauty was cold, mannered, and, when you'd seen it once, dreary. Zeus may have made wind, but he'd never broken it.

The absence of personality was nothing to do with artistic ability: the sculptors were supreme. Yet the faces of the Greek world had to wait until the Hellenistic period to have life breathed into them. With life came lines, blemishes and wear and tear, unseen before. This didn't happen in metropolitan Athens: it happened, as important things always do, at the edge.

Hellenistic art was the art of exile. People understand others only if they understand themselves, and people only understand themselves if they have a home, and often people only know they have a home, or know their home, when they're away from it. That's what happened to the exiled sculptors of the Hellenistic revolution. They said, in their wistfulness, dispossession and pain, that wistfulness, dispossession and pain are of the essence, and carved them into twisted eyebrows and deep frowns.

Theo had no face because he had no home, and therefore couldn't be properly homeless.

ΨΨΨ

All the stuff about statues mattered to Theo because it's not very nice to spend a winter in a wood when you've got no face. When you're surrounded by things that do – notably foxes, which are supremely themselves - it's rather shameful: a peculiar kind of poverty.

It would help, he thought, to look at the sea all winter. For the sea has no faces, or so many faces that it comes to the same thing.

So he abandoned his burrow and built a driftwood shack on the edge of the sea.

ΨΨΨ

The door was vaguely ecclesiastical: a Gothic arch made from the gunwales of a wrecked dinghy. The walls were pallets from a Korean container ship, with Chinese polystyrene shoved inside. On the floor was a top notch Persian carpet that had floated out of a flooded Shropshire manor house and spent a season buried in Severn mud before being disinterred by a pulse of rain. The chairs were fish boxes with stamps from Reykjavik and Bergen. The table was a door that had led to a bordello in Ouidah, and the bed a piece of foam no longer insulating a Lisbon shed.

He took as long as he could to complete the work, but soon there was no denying it was done. Then there was nothing to do but watch.

Even this is hard to do without a face, but he did his best.

Theo

So I'm a god without a face? Since your metaphors visibly snap by over-extension, I can't really be bothered to argue. But on a point of information, it's not *faces* you see for the first time in the Hellenistic period. It is *expressions* on anatomically plausible faces. The lines in the marble acknowledge and celebrate age, sun, weariness, contempt, pain, fear, lust and stress. They throw away the flattering airbrush in the fourth century BC.

Those historical facts don't map so neatly onto your theory of identity being tied up with exile, do they? And what about the contemporary faceless art of much of sub-Saharan Africa – done by people who *really* know how to live in a place, and have never, ever moved from there? As you drone on about Greek epic and the fecundity of dispossession, using the sea as the glue that sticks all your fragments together, isn't it a problem for you that the sea god both keeps Odysseus in exile and is the means of his return?

What you've left out says much more than what you've put in. I wrote haiku for the first time that autumn, for instance. I'd previously despised the genre. You don't mention that. Nor do you mention my library of leaf prints, my purchase of a dissecting microscope, my excavation of molehills, or my correspondence (c/o a small mountain monastery) with a man in a cave on Mount Athos.

There is one bit – just one bit – of restraint in this chapter. And you even draw attention to it, inviting applause for your self-knowledge, humility, and artistic reticence: I 'walked towards the sea', you write. 'It is not clear why. *There's a strong temptation to get all symbolical, and there's too much of that in this book.*' Tosser. Yet you say kind things. Thank you. I should be kind back. But I'm finding it hard.

Did you consider that I might have gone into the sea because I'd had torrential diarrhoea from eating limpets, and needed to wash my arse? You didn't, I think: stereotypes never get the shits, do they?

So it goes on. Why is the salvaged carpet more significant because it came from Shropshire (if it did: how on earth could you know that?) and was buried for a while (if it was), in Severn mud? Can't it just be a carpet without a hinterland? History is sometimes wholly irrelevant. And the waves that came to my beach: did they somehow soak up some vibes from that adulterous Portuguese couple and transmit them to the Somerset sand? Really? And if so, are you saying that the sand somehow became morally suspect? Or what? It's window-dressing, isn't it?

I note, too, your insistent personalization of things that aren't obviously personal. Your sea 'growls'. It's angry. It has a maw, and indeed we're told that that's its defining characteristic.

I assume you're trying to mount an argument for some sort of animism. If so: *argue*. Don't just *assert*. You seem to think that if you say often enough that a rock is alive intelligent people will agree with you. You underestimate your public. If you were a student you'd be out on your ear.

Which brings me to the 'dolphin'. I'm not going to start on the wild biological speculations. Let alone on the childish anthropomorphism. I'll just point out that there is a current in those parts, known to the laconic locals as 'The Teaser'. It's a narrow rip current, about twenty yards across, which sucks you straight out into the Channel. Over half way across, just as you're looking at Wales and saying your prayers, it does a hairpin turn and comes back more or less the way it came, dumping you a hundred yards from where it picked you up.

The Author

If you don't trust me, Theo, listen to the other voices.

Anyway: Like the dark, the cold crept in from the sea. The land, like a wave ending its journey, turned in on itself. Leaves curled, making fists against the chill and the black, and then gave in. The grass shrank back. A few brave, pointless flowers hung on, with no bees to be drawn to their colour, and then the colour drained away.

It's a resting: a regrouping, Theo insisted. Things have to die in order to rise. Hurrah for winter! It ensures spring. Jews and academics, being smart, know that things only really begin when the old stuff shrivels, and so they begin their years when the leaves turn.

For a while he believed his own sermon.

The belief didn't last. When the beans and pot noodles ran out he hauled fish from the sea and clubbed them. He shot rabbits and pigeons. Sometimes he wounded them and had to chop or twist their necks as they moaned or screamed. He saw winter in their eyes as they died: real, un-theologised winter: a winter he had brought. This, he saw, was the same winter that shrivelled the wood. There was no beginning in it. It was all ending. Dark and cold were dark and cold, whether they came from a 12 bore cartridge or a Siberian depression. The dead rabbit couldn't see the sun, and nor could the winter wood.

The sea doesn't have the same sort of winter as the wood. It tilts; it rearranges; it is quieter down below and rowdier up top; but for most of the sea – the deep blue – there are no real seasons: time doesn't get much further down than the red light does. You can stop the clock if you're part of the deep sea.

ψψψ

When the sea is really steep there are no flint-edged faces. The artists are wrong. There is no order or form. The Hebrews were right: the sea, when it is being itself, is chaos. It is only itself when it's furious. When it is alive it rises like Scottish fell land. Boats are sheep at the valley bottom.

Some birds need storms: the chaos is their motor. They are the real sea birds: the albatrosses and the other tubenoses. They are more birds of the sea than the others because they know that the sea doesn't stop where the water ends: it goes well up into the air above. They live with equal intensity in the sea-above-the-water and the sea-below-the-water. Lesser birds, which may dive deep (as the tubenoses do not) seek refuge in the air from the sea. They don't really know the sea-in-the-air. They're frightened of the sea when it is being itself, and so they're not proper sea-things.

Manx shearwaters slid like ball-bearings between layers of wind. Storm petrels the size of sparrows waltzed with black columns of screaming air a mile high and five miles wide.

Sometimes the sea retreated into itself, and then the water was tense and shivering or slack and flabby. Then the shelduck pattered and fussed; the gulls yawned, fieldfares and redwings from the fields behind swung in flocks over the sea, just for a change, and the auks, out at sea, killed less than usual because the fish (which normally could see quite well into the air), saw them coming. The surface fish were safer from things coming from below, for they saw the looming jaws in the mirror of the unruffled top film of the sea.

On those days, boats sputtered out from the town, packed with men in waterproofs, swollen with pies and atavistic pride. They were after bony fishes more closely related to the fishermen than the fish were to sharks – fish which could be taught to distinguish between Bach and Stravinsky and had individual preferences for one or the other.[35]

The plan was to asphyxiate or decompress the fish until their entrails burst through their mouths, and take photos for the mantlepiece. The hiss of the fish-finding sonar was like white noise at nightclub volume to the dolphin toying with seaweed just off Theo's beach. The bang of the engine was like a fist in the solar plexus to the bass whose lateral lines could pick up the rumour of an eddy from the pelvic fin of a young haddock fifty yards off.

ΨΨΨ

Behind him all was surrender and decay. He couldn't bear to look. He closed the back window of the shack so he couldn't be taken unawares. Twice a day, in the morning and after dark, he went into the sea up to his neck, and ducked his head. He didn't swim. That would have been disrespectful. Perhaps that's why Greeks don't swim. They just bob. The sea took his heat. It seemed a fair price for what it gave him.

He read fitfully, made friends with a field mouse, and noticed that the more he washed his father's shirts in the sea, the more his father's smell filled them.

He fed the crow. She watched his eyes. She brought him nuts. She got drunk on fermenting apples and staggered back to him through the air with one. She laid it at his feet and looked up at him. He looked down at her, picked up the apple, and ate it, maggots and all. The crow was pleased. So was Theo.

Limpet (*Patella vulgate*)

There are ways it might be said that a limpet on a rock on Theo's promontory was affected by him. But any such attempt would be eco-sophistry or mysticism. It would need to invoke Theo's corporate responsibility for the sins of the human race, or rely on an infinitesimal shift in the limpet's biochemistry as a result of Theo washing his tea mug in the sea, or on an irrelevantly tiny reduction in the stress of living because Theo had eaten a couple of the dog whelks that bore through limpet shells and suck them out like milk-shakes, or on a little more wiggle room on the rock because Theo, in the very early days, ate limpets himself. But any of this would depend on near-abstractions rather than real, rocky things. And since Theo has abjured abstraction, I will too.

The limpet, then, didn't know that Theo was there, and didn't care.

Yet that too is part of the story, though we will not hear again from the limpet.

The Author

Newboldt – possibly the most immoral poet there has ever been – wrote about a young officer, captured by brigands, awaiting his certain death at dawn. 'All night long, in a dream untroubled by hope/He brooded, clasping his knees.'[36]

Theo's nights were troubled by hope, and that, he thought, was cruel. Wherever he looked he saw malignant and glorious contingency. It exhausted him. He was a mouse, the universe a cat, the little brown sea a paw. The ripples on the surface of the sea had never been that way before in the entire history of things, and never would be that way again. The pillar of rock had never been that shape before, and never would be again, for wind had just taken away a grain. It had never reflected light like that before, and never would again. It was insufferable. It was exhausting. The constant newness demanded constantly new responses. The fear of the cat's paw was bad enough, but more insufferable still was the need to respond with wonder, gratitude and exhilaration. For any response would be inadequate, and wouldn't he be condemned for that? The contingency demanded, too, that he be correspondingly capable of change when he hadn't been schooled in the necessary techniques, and wouldn't have the energy to deploy them if he had. The splendid variety of the world taunted him with his own lumpenness.

Why should he put up with the taunting and the stress? He could wrong-foot the universe by a genuine act of agency. So he got up and walked into the little town where I'd been living for a while. It was there, one frosty January night, that I met him.

ΨΨΨ

I loved him from the moment I saw him, as one loves a piece of mannered porcelain – because he was so fragile. And also, I admit, because he was Greek. This was pure prejudice but prejudice based, just like our respect for the laws of nature, on a huge data set. There are no doubt mean, grey, grasping Greeks (and of course the history of twentieth century Greece amply confirms it), but I've never met them.

He was sitting at the end of the bar, his big moon-eyes flashing, drinking cider from a small glass tumbler, swinging his *komboloi* and talking to a tourist about the need to respect the Earth-Shaker.[37]

'I don't know about that', cackled the tourist, to snorting approval from red men, 'But I've a lot of respect for the Knee-Trembler.' And when Theo despised him utterly but smilingly, and didn't disembowel him with a bronze sword, I knew that I'd like him as well as love him.

Rachel

Theo is a nice man. He buys me Sprite. I think he is sad. I don't think he knows as much as other grown ups. When I ask him about anything he just says: 'I don't know' and asks me something about me. That is a bit creepy.

My dad likes him and thinks he is some sort of weird god. My dad talks to him a lot and buys him cider and afterwards writes down what he says in a little blue notebook.

Sometimes when Theo has drunk a lot of cider he talks really loud and fast and then falls over, which is really funny. He lives in a shed, but I've never been there. He has a hat made from a duck.

Theo

Rachel (an excellent, unspoilt child, by the way) has it more or less right. You're not writing about me at all. You're writing about some sort of wraith that you imbue with supernatural qualities. Do you need to *worship* so much? Is life really so dull that you have to populate it with imaginary beings, dressed up exotically and improbably? I'd thought you *were* being kind, but now I suspect you were just being kind about your own thoughts: a form of self-love. I wonder if you'd be kind about *me?*

The Author

That's rich. You've spent so much of your life doubting that there's such a thing as *you,* and now *you* want to be liked?

I will mention, though, that every three months Theo sat in a van in the little grey town, watching his blood drain into a bag. 'Take more', he said to the nurse. 'I don't need it'. She asked for a psychiatric opinion. And on his hip there was a scar where bone marrow had been sucked out for a Kurdish child.

Dolphin

The fish sank with the cold, and the dolphin sank with them. A gust of water a hundred yards deep and half a mile across blew a cloud of plankton in from the Atlantic. The cloud billowed round Lundy, and clouds of fish billowed inside and around it. The dolphin snapped and chopped and then another gust broke up the cloud and the dolphin headed back up towards the little grey town. He passed through a cone of spinning water and remembered, and what he remembered was a good thing: better than killing mackerel: better even than mating.

Chorus

And here, now, all things are coming together. There are many threads in place on the loom, and if you look you may see the start of the picture. If he will wait and let the Immortals – or perhaps that Immortal whom he loves and who loves him – weave on, then all may be well.

7. The bar

The Author

Greeks drink wine in small glasses that you hold not by a stem, but in your hand. The wine warms up to blood temperature, so that when you drink it it's a transfusion of your own heat back to your body or, if the wine glass is a body (which many say it is) a transfusion from one body to another.

In the bar by the quay in the little grey town by the little brown sea, Theo drank his cider like that, in a glass bought in Sparta.

Averaged out over the course of a lifetime, he lived the Aristotelian life of equipoise.

That's not much of an achievement, in fact. So did the Dionysiac maenads, for they, remember, came back to their tidy suburbs after copulating with the horned god and rending things limb from limb. They resumed their workaday WI lives, baking cakes and chairing committees, and being so respectable that they mitigated their wildness down to a golden mean which would have made Aristotle glad.

There were whole hours at a time, though, when Theo lived the right, thriving life; when Apollo and Dionysus sat beaming at one another. This was when he played his bouzouki in the bar every Tuesday night, between songs about lecherous highwaymen and dead farmers - and on his own in his shed, looking out past the ships to the winking lights of Wales and on to Piraeus and Nicosia. They liked him in the bar, despite their instinctive xenophobia, and though he was impossible to patronize. They listened to him as you listen to *lieder* – understanding not a word; drunk on the cadences; suspecting that the cadences related exactly to the meaning; too drunk on cadence and cider to know that they were being condemned or lampooned.

And Theo preached. By Poseidon, did he preach. Set pieces: blustering, bigoted, cynical and vigilant - for he was straining to hear the occasional notes in his own register.

'Most people here', said he, 'want to live in a mortuary: clinical cream carpets, uncluttered white walls; toilets where complex and beautiful dung-creatures are poisoned with chemicals. I suppose to want to live as you'll die is a perverted kind of consistency.'

'But you only see it in benighted Protestant cultures', he went on. 'There even the secular want their churches to be as arid as their IKEA living rooms and their dying-rooms and their dead-rooms. But go into a Greek Orthodox church. You won't see a square inch of wall. Everything's covered with attempts, however pathetic and doomed, to understand God. There are paintings of saints – the witnesses to what the Church says is the truth - and of the God-man, and divine light done in gold leaf and vegetable pigments. The Orthodox know that eyes aren't enough, so they shake frankincense at your nose. And that eyes and noses aren't enough, so they sing everything at you in tunes 1500 years old that break your heart if you've still got one. And that eyes and noses and ears aren't enough, so they hug you and push you to your knees. And that eyes and noses and ears and touch aren't enough, so they buy the best wine from the Peloponnese to be God's blood, and everything's an excuse for a cake or a spitted lamb. And that eyes and noses and ears and touch and taste aren't enough, so they have scripture and argument and poetry and the liturgy of St. John Chrysostom which is all those things, and so on a Sunday morning in London you can hear the flies buzzing round the loincloth of the thief at Calvary who soiled himself as the nail went through his ulnar nerve, and smell the sweat and the thyme on the hill as a Jewish goatherd wondered if he could still say the *Shema* if Jesus were Yahweh.

'The big white spaces in the toilets and the churches of the well-scrubbed northern Protestants purport to declare that God is too big to be tied down to word or image. Of course He's too bloody big. But that means He's too big not to make His presence felt everywhere, not that He's too big to make His presence felt at all. They've misunderstood Plato. He didn't say that those shadows on the cave wall could tell us *nothing* about the things that cast them. Just that you shouldn't come to final conclusions on the basis of limited information. As Paul, that Jew-to-the-Greeks who became the Greek-to-the-Jews pointed out, we see as through a glass, darkly. Not that we don't see anything at all, or that it's pointless to try to see more'.

Anyway', concluded Theo, 'that's why it's demonic to have a cream carpet.'

'Hurrah for the Greek', shouted Ken.

'Quite right', agreed Burt.

'What are you drinking?' asked Steve.

'The usual', said Theo. 'Don't mind if I do.'

'I've been to Mykonos', said Ken. 'Great place. Great shags. Food crap. Met a girl called Mandy. Bought her a dress and she left me for the waitress.'

'Who's it all for?' I asked Theo. He looked at me as if I were mad.

ΨΨΨ

At the end of each evening he bowed to the bar, touched an imaginary hat, and walked out into the night. There he always found reproach. Whether it came from the sea, the shore, the wood, or himself he was never sure. But it was now the main force that drove him. He saw that the wild did everything better.

The owl killed faster and more silently than even Steve said he had killed in Oman. The sandpipers were more Celtic than the pipes and fiddles. The foxes were more lusty and more faithful than Ken. The night interrogated Theo harder and more intelligently than the retired High Court judge who had backed Theo into a corner one night and gone acerbically, syllable by syllable, through everything he had said. The wind in the ferns was more lascivious than the most bosomy barmaid. The sea made him ache more than he ached when his bar stool sermons were misunderstood. At its worst the night enshrined human virtues better than the bar at its best.

He ran back to the bar each night, desperate for rest and relief from his rumination; desperate for the sound of his own crass voice, his safe, conservative anarchy, his jokes, his disciples, his unrecognized double-entendres, and the glass with his name on it. Out there in the dark it was pure and old and continually new; it demanded so much. One day it would demand everything. He was too tired for the rigours of the dark. He despised himself for his tiredness, and despised the disciples for not despising him.

There were, he reasoned, two ways to deal with this. One was to man up and become a beast – a proper, balanced, clean beast, happy in the night. He wasn't up to that. The other – a temporary option – was to find someone who would hold him in the contempt in which he held himself. It would make for a relationship more honest than anything else he had.

ψψψ

One night in early February a candidate for this second solution presented herself at the bar.

She, like the dark, was both very old and very young: sharp, hard, hurt, seventeen, without illusions (and not keen to acquire any) and so incapable of disillusionment. She'd told her careers master, in bed, that she wanted lots of money, and didn't care how she got it. Once said, she presumed it was true. She had nice legs, an IQ of 145, and a philosophy and vocabulary lifted unedited from *Marie Claire*. Self-examination, whether of breasts or psyche was, she was fond of saying, for the dateless, desperate, and unwaxed.

She arrived as Theo was starting a sermon.

' "Creatures, I give you yourselves,"' says the lion Aslan in *The Magician's Nephew*. Most of us say 'No thanks.'

It was a promising start. His congregations settled comfortably on their stools. Then, over her vodka and tonic, the girl said: 'But Aslan's a fictional pussy cat, isn't he? Why should we listen to him?'

'It's a metaphor', said Ken, carefully.

'Yeah: a metaphor', agreed Steve. 'Carry on'.

The girl wouldn't be deflected. 'What does it mean to have yourself given to you? And how can we say no? It's bullshit. Isn't it?'

This was directed straight at Theo, who looked into his glass, half-smiling.

Everyone looked at him. After an age he looked up at the girl and murmured, still with the half-smile: 'It may be.'

There was a collective sigh. Everyone was disappointed. They'd hoped for a terminal put-down. Ken hurried to retrieve the situation.

'Course it's not. It means that we make bad choices. Like', he added nervously, looking to Steve for support, 'wearing shoes like that in a place like this.'

The girl ignored him. She held Theo's gaze and licked her lips.

Theo's silence, and the joke about the shoes, made it impossible for the audience to stay. They drank up quickly, made excuses, and went out into the cold. The barmaid went to change a barrel, leaving Theo and the girl facing each other at opposite ends of the bar.

'We can go now' said the girl at last. He followed her out.

ᚢᚢᚢ

She was, he found in the morning, the daughter of the judge who had cross-examined him in the pub. She had an unexceptionable and irrelevant English name. She was staying in her father's huge, ugly house, buried in the hill above the harbour. Her father was rarely there. A Restoration aristocrat with the girl's eyes hunted stags in a park at the foot of her bed. Other relatives in gilt frames watched the pair without surprise or judgment as they undressed or circled one another.

Most of the rooms looked out over the Severn Sea. The skirr and bang of the sea shuddered round them. Salt frosted the ancestral beards and corroded the halberds and pikes. Gulls cackled at the decay and threw up on the window sills.

The girl had locked the doors leading to these rooms. She kept the keys on a chain round her neck even when all her clothes were on the floor.

Her bedroom looked out on the hill. Its tiny window framed a patch of soil, too dark for plants. The sun rose later and set earlier in the room.

The girl wouldn't go to the beach. She couldn't. When she walked to the shops she took a roundabout way that meant she never looked at the sea, and she was plugged into music from Nevada that overwhelmed the sound of the swell.

ᛣᛣᛣ

Since he'd reached his beach, Theo had only rarely eaten animals. This was because animal-eating was morally serious. It was, in proper evolutionary perspective, an act of near cannibalism. A cow appeared in his family album only a few pages back. Any half-reflective person, he said, would think twice before sinking his teeth into the buttocks of a dead cousin.

This wasn't an absolute prohibition. But only very intense pleasure could justify eating a cousin, and very intense pleasure was by its nature, very occasional.

It had been similar with sex. He was no monk, and had had his moments in sacramental places and at sacramental times: in a field of standing stones on a May morning, say, or at the back of the college chapel, or when he was out of his mind with fear. But he knew that he was entering gods - eternally enduring things - and that they ripped part of him away as payment for the entry.

There was also this: Once you've seen your mother bayoneted, you'll never uncomplicatedly penetrate a woman.

He withdrew each time with a wheeze of apology and a lugubrious sense of history which a less scrupulous man might have hammed up into a reputation for being deep and sensitive. So until that first night with the girl he was constitutionally virginal. He'd done the act, but that was all. He'd never been present. He hadn't dared. He'd been too much in awe of the dark and dazzling metaphysics of copulation.

But the girl had told him to be there with her, and he had complied, and much of him had been taken into her and would not now be easily returned.

They ate chops and brains and no potatoes and went to the dark room in the hill. Because lots of him was being taken, he assumed that the girl must not only be a god, like the other women had been, but a particularly potent one. That kept him diligently in her bed.

There's nothing personal about this, he sometimes told himself. It is union not with a person, but with an ecosystem; a dynasty. How else can I get in touch with the Eighteenth century? Those severe women in their powdered wigs live on between the shapely legs of this, their descendant. What responsible scholar would pass up such an opportunity to travel in time and hobnob with the dead? This was fieldwork, not fornication. The only morality involved was the moral imperative of investigation.

A week went past. He never went to the bar or to his shed by the sea. He looked at the girl from all angles, and at the square of earth through the bedroom window, and when the girl let him, read and re-read the book (Seferis[38]) that had been in his pocket on the night he had met her. He washed his pants in the bath, heard the gulls through the walls, watched the ancestors watching him, and was eroded.

Another week: no bar, no shed. Bed; earth; distant gulls; shirt. Less and less of him. Seferis unbearable. Heaps of hot offal and no veg.

Another week. They were sitting at the table and their eyes were hot and red and the steaming liver was more raw than ever and she chewed and he saw the liver in her teeth and a pile of plates lifted from a shelf and hurled itself six feet across the room through the cloud of liver steam and she should have screamed but did no such thing but paused with her fork in her mouth, looked at the rubble and carried on eating. When she had finished her mouthful she nodded at a cupboard.

'There's a brush in there.'

Next morning a cup narrowly missed her head and smashed on the wall behind. In the afternoon the Collected Works of Walter Scott were swept onto her shoulders as she unbuttoned her shirt. At night a stuffed owl sprang from its perch, through its glass case and onto her lap, and at dawn Theo dressed silently as she slept and ran as fast as he could, back to the sea.

ΨΨΨ

It is not true that the sea is without form. Water does not significantly deform with pressure. It always has shape. It always self-sculpts. Even when it is not colliding with a rock or a whale, it is colliding, at least at a molecular level, with itself. It makes its own waves. It is always starting something new. You never step into the same river twice, observed Heraclitus. Nor do you step twice into the same sea.

Since he had last been there, the sea by his shed had had an almost infinite number of iterations – of rolling drafts. Between them they said something about the sea, but no one of them *was* the sea. Nor was a vast archive of drafts the sea.

Theo ran down the beach and dived head first and fully clothed into a streaming constellation of stories. They clung to him then span away from him as he swam down into the kelp forest and dripped from him as his head broke the surface and as he scrambled out and shook himself like a dog. He changed, filled his rucksack, and ran into town to catch a bus.

Carrion Crow

Since the crow was made mainly of habit and landscape, and because Theo was part of its landscape and the subject of some of its habits, the crow noticed that he had gone.

At first this was just an observation – tied to the crow's survival software – like noticing that a branch has moved, and it made the crow cautious. But the crow wasn't a survival machine, or a machine of any kind. She had to survive to be what she was, but please, you white-coated pipette-wielders, don't confuse means with ends.[39] It doesn't begin to follow that she was what she was only in order to survive. She remembered kindly thrown crusts which she neither liked nor needed, and liked the kindness without thinking that it might give her something to eat. She saw in the man's face that he could be trusted not to wring her neck, break her leg or fill the air with noise and hail from a thunderstick.

So she hopped to the shed door and put her head first to one side, and then to another, which would have given a human the impression of pondering; of consideration. That would have been wrong: she was only trying to get the full visual picture. The pondering came in the stillness that followed.

She hammered at the door with a friendly beak designed for ripping and stabbing. All she wanted now was company and the pattern she knew. Though her best pickings came from change, destruction, and corruption, she liked the old, kind, warm un-change of the shed.

It was neither kind nor warm now, and she was disconcerted. Her learned preference for kindness and warmth might well look like the morality – or at least the decent behaviour – of a well-brought-up child. Who is to say they are different?

Each stab at the door was an insistent kiss. After an hour or so the kisses wore a hole in the door, and the crow pushed through. In the shed she found clothes and a bed. They smelt of the man. Her tongue was fibrous, with few taste receptors, but she dragged it over the bed, and the bed was sour as the air was not. She defaecated on the pillow to show that she felt at home and because the man would want to know she had visited.

The shed was cold. It had not been so cold when the man was there. The crow noticed this. She came close to being metaphorical: to identifying physical warmth with emotional warmth. The nearly-metaphorical bird climbed onto the cover of *Zorba the Greek,* pushed out a pellet glittering with beetles, and squeezed back through the kiss-hole onto the shore.

Eel

Every night when he came back from the bar, Theo stood on a rock near the shed and urinated thunderously into the sea. The eel's crack was immediately below.

On her snout, in front of her eye, were pits lined with cells so sensitive that she could detect ten molecules of urea. Urea was interesting. It was released by potential prey when they voided into the sea and when they were torn by other predators. It made the eel's heart beat faster. Her tail beat reflexively and thrust her out from the crack, jaws grinding.

After a few pints of cider, Theo would expel billions of urea molecules, and (for it was proper cider, from old trees), aromatic phenols whose benzene rings bowled like cartwheeling clowns into the eel's olfactory pits.

The immense nightly overload desensitized the eel. She was a poorer, thinner hunter that winter. When she was deluged she felt as if her gums were pulled back from her teeth, just as you feel when you drink very tannic red wine. Her teeth seemed sharper and longer, but she was less able to do anything with them.

Chorus

And now he is away; gone to seek healing for the wound we all bear, or will. Gone to wash in the river that flows down from Cape Tenaros to the grey-lands; the fast-flowing river of blood.

8. Looking for Mother and Father

The Author

Theo's mother and father, being dead, were now wild, and he went into the wild to look for them.

His reasoning went like this: The vibrations of a chisel decide the shape of a statue. The way that atoms vibrate decide what a substance actually *is*. If you set something vibrating it never completely stops. Its ripples continue for ever, and go everywhere. So it is not ridiculous to seek past events. Even millions of miles away.

He wanted to hug his mother. He wanted to upbraid his father for dying so inconsiderately. He wanted to see how they both looked now that they were wild. He wanted to be soaked in the antiseptic that was his father, and so be free of the infection that was the girl. His father smelt always of aftershave and incense. If his father had met the girl it would have been all right. He would have decontaminated her. His aftershave would have neutralized the contagion. Demons would have run screaming from the incense.

It wasn't too late! His father could still meet the girl and, though he had gone wild, he no doubt still smelt the same, and would still clean her up.

ΨΨΨ

The first bus went to Bristol. The second to Sheffield. The third to his old house. He walked up the drive. There was someone at home. The television flickered. Someone in a suit was giving away money for the answers to moronic questions. The toilet coughed. By a bin bag at the back door he found a thin shard of his seventh birthday party. Under a rosemary bush was a vague piece of old, bad news. Stuck on a birch tree was half a bedtime story from when the night was soft and yellow against his face and his mother's face was close to his. Beeswax prayer candles shivered in the wind from the moor.

His animals seemed more enduring than his parents, which was a kind of blasphemy: a rabbit nose twitched by the back wall, next to a pair of ears. There was a smell of hay; but no aftershave, no knotted silk cravat, and no click of beads.

He sat in the garden and waited for them as they had waited for him outside schools, dentists and examination halls. At eleven the TV was switched off. His parents would have liked that. Not knowing how these things worked, it made him hopeful that they would come. But the fragments skittered away. The candles blew out. It was as if the past were parasitic on the present: as if it had to be powered by the electricity pouring into the TV or along the neurones of the new occupants.

He sat until his fingers were blue and his lips white, then stood up and shuffled up the road towards the heather.

ᚦᚦᚦ

He lodged for a week in a cavity in one of the Edge's teeth, looking out over the places the wild kids had staked out and stalked: the battered farms, the rolling ridges, the high black tops, the low black woods; fields where mist was trapped by dry stone walls and never escaped to the next field; stones and tremulous altars; bus shelters where his father had sat in state with a pork pie; barns where bedtime story dragons had been chained; rivers with flotillas of drowned bats with primly folded wings; coverts paced by pheasants whose instincts were Himalayan and royal; shops selling pigs' cheese and snakes in gin and moorhens for roasting and witches' toenails and velvet-covered rubber rings for barristers with piles.

He heard the wind from Manchester, the clink of karabiners, the panting and grinding of a couple in the cotton grass, the grumbling of lorries taking sheep to be killed, the thud of water on his coat, the crumpling of the wrappers on his chocolate bars, the whooping and screaming of food on the merry-go-round of his ileum, and his breath – the first one of which had been a cause of such relief to his mother and such surprise to his father (who had seen it as the first of many lamentable declarations of independence).

He smelt the yoghurt breath of grouse, the sweet belches of cows, diesel fumes, a tropical sea with trilobites, and the cold, which has its own smell. He was swaddled in fog which dissolved everything it touched and so filled him when he breathed with steak and kidney pie, lichen from asbestos chicken houses, the dandruff of starlings, the varnish from the cover of the *New Testament in Scots* (left in a skip in Castleton), the lice of the resident kestrel and the scurf of a passing buzzard. In the day scent rose out of the land, bringing some of the land with it. It lapped at his feet by mid-morning. By lunchtime he was chest-deep in the land five hundred visual yards below him, and it was over his head by three. Then it ebbed back down into its soil and reeds and ditches, leaving a tideline across his shoulders.

In an excited synaesthetic moment, somewhere between sleep and waking, he thought he had seen the smell of aftershave, and heard the cravat, and smelt the beads swinging. But he was never sure, and if they were there at all, they were gone with the next parcel of wind. Just because something was wild didn't mean, apparently, that it was present in all wildness.

Tawny owl (*Strix aluco*)

During the day the owl clutched the same beech branch that its father and grandfather had clutched. Its claws nearly met in the soft wood. If it faced forward, it would have looked straight down into the dead father's garden. But its head could turn through nearly a full circle, and it always faced away, towards the moor. Daylight was shrill, hot, hard and vulgar. It pinched its lids against the noise, the pain, and the fuss. The lids opened and shut at the same pace as the falling and rising sun. In the dark it could see a vole's split ends at fifty yards and hear the bile leak into a mouse's duodenum. The TV had been an abomination, like high-explosive shells whizzing and screaming and crashing. The owl stayed only out of loyalty to the branch. There was nothing to eat in the garden. There never had been. The gardens on either side throbbed with food, but the food never came through the holes in the fence.

The Author

So, having failed to find his parents in Sheffield, the obvious thing to do was to look in Greece – where they'd always said he could find the most salubrious of unseen places, and where he'd managed to see that stone on the Acropolis hill. He did the obvious thing.

He went by train, first of all, afraid of approaching Greece too fast, and hiding in the toilet when the ticket collectors did their rounds. He was stunned, drugged and apologetic; jumping at every sound though his ears were plugged with wax: revolted by the violence of the plunging pistons, the pound and burp of the engines and the casualness of the passengers; their lack of any sense of occasion – the main occasion being the extraordinary fact that they existed, against all the odds.

Fearful of lies, he turned away from screens and newsagents at the Gare du Nord. He was happier when he got to Italy, whose language he didn't know. He stood in the rain outside the Porta Garibaldi station in Milan with the antiseptic wild pouring over him.

It wasn't until he stumbled out of the Venice central railway station in the early morning dark and heard the slop of brine on the rotting quay that he remembered, suddenly and happily, that the girl hated and feared the sea.

ᚹᚹᚹ

Everyone admires Venice. But it is a dubious sort of admiration – an admiration of hubris, engineering, uniqueness and improbability.

Her beauty is borrowed: most of it from Byzantium. If you're seduced into rhapsodies on the Venetian light, remember that the light on the sea would be just the same if the city weren't there. The city's just a perch from which you can see what would otherwise be invisible to humans.

'There's more dignity in a single dive of a grebe in the lagoon' (he wrote in his notebook as he sat looking out towards Cemetery Island, clinking glasses with himself rather than with his dad, who hadn't turned up, and watching the *vaporetti* tunnel through the fog) 'than in all the vaulting, vaulted piazzas. With the most improbable forbearance the city might make it to the irrelevantly tiny age of fifteen hundred years. Then it'll dissolve into the sea. For its last five hundred years it will be propped up humiliatingly on beams as a human invalid is propped up on a frame. Steel gates, like incontinence pads, will keep it dryer than it would otherwise be. No one can seriously pretend, however gorgeous their robes or their self-drafted history, that they're the lord of the place. Even now the waves come in when they want. They swill over the carpets, the mosaics and the marble sixty times a year. Give up the pretence, poor Venice. Your only success is not being submerged for a few years (not enough years to alter significantly the shape of a grebe's web) and convincing day trippers with selfie sticks that you're not on the run all the time. Clap, clap, clap.'

Other fragments from this time verge on the psychotic. Any one of them would have made any half-competent psychiatrist reach for the prescription pad, if not the phone to the secure unit.

'A gull sicks up the indigestible bits of its prey within six hours. The hoi polloi buried in Venice's cemetery island have a decade there before the island sicks them up and their bones are mixed in a communal pit. If you're a rich Venetian you might be able to wait in your grave until an earthquake disgorges you or the winds creep through a crack and blow your dust into the lagoon. In a poorly drained churchyard the worms might be through your pine coffin in five years or so, with a fair chance of you, in the form of a worm, being eaten by a gull, and turned into a regurgitated pellet not long after that. In a municipal crematorium you'll be disgorged in a bolus of smoke within a quarter of an hour (half an hour if there's a queue) to be inhaled by schoolchildren and mice, and so eaten and disgorged again for ever.'

'I started the process of dissolution early. That Turkish wound was crawling with maggots. I suppose they've just kept on feeding.'

'Charles Lamb asked 'Who, in similar circumstances, has not been tempted to exclaim with Charoba, in the poem of Gebir: Is this the mighty ocean? is this all?'[40] Well, I haven't, for a start'.

But though, or because, the notebook was depressing, he was as blithe as a piglet in clean straw.

He had his beard trimmed and perfumed by a Syrian with a theatrical limp. He sauntered when the sun shone and slouched when it rained. He loved the sewage, the teetering garrets, and the open yet gentle contempt in which he and everyone else were held by the Venetians. He loved the white homeless birds, the twisted stone faces, the girls' calves, the rope, the paint, the tar, the thump of boats, the rise and fall of the jetties like diaphragms keeping air in the city, the olives on the tideline of the islands, the prissy little glasses with pink fizz held in huge hands. He went promptly at five to six every evening to the only stool in the peeling *bacaro* whose stale air still contained the last wheeze of the fresco painter (a specialist in cherubs) who'd been stabbed there for philandry some time in the sixteenth century.

Something whooped at night across the water, and he smiled. Stucco slid off the face of his apartment, weed slid up the steps towards the *fondamenta,* waves slapped the city's stilts and made it rock, lobsters howled in the kitchens, barnacles on the boats pursed their craggy lips and sucked soup, the dead in their soggy coffins rose and sank with the tide. Crowds hustled off the cruise ships and their weight pressed the city further into the mud: it tilted as they surged towards St. Mark's. Corks from Portuguese oaks, full of Atlantic salt, hilariously shattered chandeliers. Cannon-balls that had crashed through mediaeval rigging and were now worn to the size of blueberries rolled alongside snail shells and toothpaste tubes. A mad-eyed shearwater, fouled with oil, flapped, foundered, and pillowed its head on a beer can; squid squirted between sunken arches like herds of headless brides trailing their white trains. Rumanian kids, expecting nothing, played American songs too fast on broken accordions, their mothers too tired to look pathetic.

If you'd put your head into the sea on the east side of the Lido you wouldn't have heard (though it was deafening to creatures with subsonic hearing) the rumbling of a fin whale off the coast of Croatia. Three days ago it had nosed around off Patras, getting a bellyful of carrier bags, before turning north because its grandparents had gone that way a couple of centuries before. Off Albania it nudged a trawler; off Montenegro it ripped a net and a remora hitched a ride. It played with the Adriatic islands as if they were swings and slides, and then, bored and lonely, it surfaced, wallowed in the fog and boomed.

The boom made the plates on the sides of Trieste shrimps rattle; mackerel squealed; the squid stopped their procession up the aisle and hung in the water, holding watery breaths; planktonic flagellae fluttered in the sound-breeze, and the membranes of a billion billion cells trembled. The boom bounced back from the baffle of the Lido, over to Croatia and back and back again like a ping-pong ball. It boinged between the islands and was off towards Africa. It squeezed through the Straits of Messina, headed due west (much smaller now, and reducing all the time), just made it through the Straits of Gibraltar, and was caught by a fast northerly current which swept it (now a low growl) through the Bay of Biscay, past Land's End, and slung it (as a whisper) onto the beach below Theo's hut.

Sitting on his bar stool in Cannaregio, Theo was nearer the sea than he had been in the hut. It washed underneath and around him. It was in the grapes as it had not been in the cider apples. It was in the edginess, the disreputability, the formality (the manners were a re-action to the chaos of the waves and the exigencies of salt), the cor-rosion, and the vertigo. This was a more serious sea; hungrier, older, with more conspicuous conquests, more famous bones rattling down below, criss-crossed by shoals of archetypes. Odyssean Ithaca wasn't so far from the bar stool. And here Theo was completely safe from the girl.

Safe enough from her, but not really near the sea, though he breathed it and it settled like sweat on his skin and spun in his head. The sea, like a fox, is only seen when it wants to be seen. Like hap-piness, the harder you try to approach it, the more elusive it is.

Just as you cannot look directly at the sun, you cannot look directly at the sea. Nor can the sea be approached directly. There are many beings that can only be seen – if they can be seen at all - at the edge of vision, and often at the cusp of the day and the night. The sun cannot itself be seen, but by it everything else is seen. Similarly with the sea: without it nothing is understood.

ᛦᛦᛦ

Theo trundled out of Venice, into the sweaty toe of the Adriatic sock, and on into Trieste, that most ambiguous and duplicitous of cities - always muttering and spying - and down the coast of Croatia, which was polite and constipated. There were big red ramparts against the sea. The fish died quietly. Even the cephalopods didn't struggle so much. The sand might just as well have been scented for all the good it was doing. The paint on the jetties didn't flake. The anemones waved in the pools as though they were signaling across a library. Inland it was too green.

The hubris of the land barely faded all the way through Montenegro, and then there was Albania: shaggy, cruel, wildly kind, astringent and gnarled. A column of black sea-smoke rose into the sky, shrimps kicked, an octopus watched and considered.

Tirana, Gjirokastra, and then Greece, where it was all sea, right down to the roots of the old olives and the webbed feet of the rocks.

And there, in the centre of Athens, just off Syntagma, at a dusty table next to a demolition site, under a mask of Dionysus, that most terrestrial of gods, on the third monkey-can of red wine, the sea surged in, bringing with it dancing fish and immortal terrors and the crash and groan of ages, and his sainted father, hand in hand with his sainted mother, both smiling in the surf, and dragging Theo with them.

ΨΨΨ

And the hot sea of Greece coiled and nibbled and gnashed, and the little brown sea, cold and thick with soil, rose and dived and licked, and birds, which no one can understand, looked down on the sea for food, and this was all as it had been.

ΨΨΨ

There was no need to stay, and so he didn't. There was no need, either, to hug the coast or squeeze a shell or a starfish. So he flew direct to Heathrow in a tube of flatus, and walked for a week along screeching and mumbling roads, sleeping in hedges with shredded tyres and in barns with sick owls and barrels of engine oil, and in a B and B in Dorset with pink nylon sheets and porcelain gnomes, back to the little brown sea, nearer to being a man than he had been since he was five.

Theo

Your characters, from eels to lovers, are pre-pubertal: unformed: flat. Why bother with them at all?

I think I know why, and you don't come out of it well. You're *using* them, just as callously as the utilitarians you say you despise, as means rather than ends.

Why not give the 'girl' a name? She wasn't and isn't a girl. She's a woman, and her name, for the record, is Sarah. She has a history – and hence a present. She has parents who themselves have names. She had a childhood bedroom that looked out on a field, a pony called Toffee, and she started cutting herself at twelve when her beloved grandmother died. She read English at Edinburgh, and her poignant and eloquent dissertation on John Donne was bound and on the shelf above the bed that so obsesses you. Don't use her and then throw her away. It's not good literature, good manners, or good ethics.

And this obsession with *events*! It's exhausting. So much has to happen, and it all has to *signify*, and signify immediately. Quite apart from making your text a sort of ponderous, portentous John Buchan, it denotes a philosophy I think you'd disown if pressed: that events are the significant things: that we are what happens to us.

On style: Buchan does it so much better. To make something into a story it's not enough simply to squirt a bit of Gothic over it, or list the activities of lots of actors and then say to the reader: 'Right, connect them if you want: I can't be bothered.'

Oh: and I got a bus from Heathrow. Sorry. I know it's not so romantic.

The Author

People might well be more than their events. They're not less. And events matter. They illuminate the actors.

Using people? Hardly. You might as well say that the nineteenth century cynically used the people who happened to live then.

A bus from Heathrow? Really?

Night 1: a field outside Farnborough. You lifted up a corrugated iron sheet, disturbing a family of slow-worms and a mummified mouse in a skein of spider silk. You propped the sheet on a bag of pignuts, ate a bar of chocolate, crawled under the sheet and were asleep by eight. A toad squatted in your hat.

Night 2: somewhere on the Downs, east of Winchester, sleepless because, according to the notebook, you were lying on a bole of flint, breathing chalk dust through a dock leaf, and for some reason wouldn't move. You were on the windiest place for miles around. There were snug, dark, holes in a mediaeval beech forest just down the hill.

It was a perverse choice of bed. It might have had something to do with the yellow eyes of a white, high-stepping deer that lived in the wood.

Night 3: The New Forest, in a gorse stockade whose coconut scent swelled to sickliness as fog came down and squashed the scent to the ground.

A leech with thirty two pairs of eyes and a colour scheme that had inspired Victorian scarf-designers[41] looped along through the wet grass from a nearby pond and hung raffishly from your ear-lobe.

Night 4: Somewhere in deep Dorset (why is Dorset always deeper than the surrounding counties?), next to a track running up to a tumbledown barn. Cushioned happily in old hay and aromatic dung, but rattled out of sleep by ghost carts.

Off, scared, to the pink B and B with the gnomes.

Night 5: The Somerset Levels: swinging a flattened otter, you walked through most of the night, kicking egrets out of the rushes. A swan exploded from a flooded field and crashed into the moon. A fox on a fence held its brush like a tightrope walker's pole. Tench, like green pigs in mucous overcoats, pouted in the dark and scratched their backs on lily-stalks. Sleep at last, just before dawn, in one of the few dry ditches, head on a bottle of antifreeze, body on the old entrance-hall carpets of a Bridgewater cafe that had got too classy for golden swirls in easy-clean polyamide; feet on an Iron Age plank, pickled in sea and peat-water, which had borne the jewelled shoes of merchants bringing glass beads from Spain, and the bare feet of criminals led out to be strangled in the marsh.

Night 6: The shed: it was a terrible mess. The wind had prised up a corner of the roof and centrifuged the books and papers. They were pressed tightly to the edges of the room, as if trying to escape.

You stripped the bed, which was covered in bird shit, and flung yourself down. When you woke, both sides of the crow were watching you.

Rachel

My dad said that Theo went away. I didn't notice because I didn't see much of him anyway. But then he was in the pub one day when we went there for Coke and he looked heavier but not fatter and kept scratching his ear and didn't talk so much but smiled a bit more and he said he had an otter skin which he'd show me but I said I didn't want to see it because I liked otters and it would make me sad. He told me I should be nice to my mum and dad and I said I was anyway and he said perhaps I could teach him how to be nice to his. He asked me if I was work in progress like he was and I didn't know what he meant then either but I told my teacher and my teacher said that I shouldn't talk to him any more.

Chorus

And here he is, back with himself and with his parents on the shore of the sea – though it is not a little sea, nor a brown sea. And here should be the ending, for all that is necessary has been accomplished. Not all that might be, but do not overstretch.

9. The bullet

The Author

It was still winter when Theo returned. For weeks there was thin, brittle sun. The air at the tips of the twigs cracked. The edge of the sea curdled.

The auks were still alone, out on the deep sea, rocking in grey troughs. There was no loneliness like theirs. From time to time they'd see another of their kind round the corner of a wave, and nod, dip and turn away, even if they'd come from the same oviduct. Beneath them, in water swollen with the cold, big things nosed, swinging from side to side.

Though they had breast muscles like rump steaks, the wings of the razorbills flickered in a blur as they whirred between the furrows. It was impossible for their wings to move as fast as they did.

To deal with the fear of the hugeness of the sea they thought of grass on cliff ledges, and strands of weed, and, when it was all too much, pushed their head under their wings and tried to forget about yellow-beaked death from above and grey-toothed death from below. The death from below was the worst, because it slid. Sliding is bad; whether in water, sand or wood; worse than swooping; a badness compounded by the silence. A life deserves a whoop, or at least a cackle.

As long as it is the life of a biggish thing, that is. Or perhaps a biggish thing with eyelids and sophisticated thermoregulation.

When it's cold on land, it always feels warmer in the water. Those cold-water swimmers you think are hard or mad are enjoying themselves. That was one of the reasons why Theo, when he woke, waded into the forest of wrack just off his rock, pushing through as you push past those bead curtains in Chinese restaurants and sank in up to his neck – the bladders insulating him; an all-round duvet that stood upright.

Dolphin

On the other side of the forest someone – a dolphin - was idling in a sea-lane to see what he might kill, pulling cold air into his lungs through the top of his head; sleek and mathematical.

He turned his head, made a click in a bag, forced the click through a dome of fat to amplify it,[42] and spat it through his forehead into the kelp forest. Almost at once clicks bounced back. He felt the forest in his jaw and the jaw shuddered. Out of the shudder an image resolved - but not as we understand an image. A hundred thousand bladders waved on their twigs. The dolphin knew the width of each of their walls; saw the tube-worms squeezing along the boughs.

In a glade he saw a man with things being squeezed along inside him, and saw again, in the core of the man, the crumpled wad which sent back a storm of clicks.

The dolphin did for Theo what he had learned from his own mother. He parted the undergrowth with its nose, moved gently up to Theo, and tapped him again and again in the chest.

The Author

Theo assumed that the animal had some nasty neurological condition. Didn't sheep with scrapie sometimes press their heads against a wall? No doubt it was something like that.

He stroked it with the cautious pity you give to dying things – the pity that denies solidarity. It pushed against his hand and went back to pushing against his chest. This was uncomfortable. The discomfort wasn't just physical. It was all rather embarrassing. There were proprieties to be observed. He was a man; the dolphin was not. You couldn't just forget that. If anyone should be taking the initiative, it was him.

Dolphin

It seemed strange to the dolphin that the man didn't just dip his head and see the hard squashed thing next to his heart. Was the man stupid? The dolphin had always thought that humans were reasonably intelligent – if rather limited – creatures. Perhaps this man was different. Perhaps he had some sort of brain problem. He had seen dolphins like that: dolphins with advanced Alzheimer's disease who wouldn't feed themselves but just rocked quietly in the shallows, or who couldn't remember the shape of a magnetic field in an underwater valley, or panicked at the sight of a porpoise.[43] And dolphins with toxoplasma[44] encephalitis caused by infected cat shit washed into the sea, drunk and dozy, limp on one side. And a dolphin hit by a propeller, its brain boiling up out of its skull.

Poor man. Well, the dolphin had done its best. There was only so much you could do.

The Author

It takes a while to know that a person has really been lost. It is so outrageous that it's hard to believe that the world could behave so badly. And *all* people are so plainly meant to endure that to accept that they do not demands a massive philosophical adjustment – an adjustment so strenuous that it's impossible when you're crying or burning papers or talking to lawyers or trying to sell the house.

Then, quite suddenly, the house is sold and the lawyers have crept back into wherever it is lawyers come from, and the only fact is the fact of absence. The bigger the crowd around you, the more inescapable the absence. We all refer everything back to our living parents for comment, even when they're a thousand miles away. When they're *no* number of miles away, we notice. How can we have a conversation with *anyone* without our father whispering lovingly wrongheaded suggestions into our ear? Our riposte in every conversation has always been a reaction to our father's suggestion. If there are no ludicrous suggestions, we fall silent and everyone thinks we're dull or depressed.

It's different when you're outside and on your own. It's not that there are no people around to remind you that your parents aren't there. It is more as if your parents are there after all: as if they can live on in trees and clouds in a way that they can't stick to bricks or glass. And if you jump into the sea the pain of bereavement abates for a while. That's not because the pain of the cold or the fear of an overwhelming wave makes you forget. Not at all. It's because your parents have gone into solution. Didn't Theo's mother and father come out of the surf?

This is bordering on madness.

What began to worry Theo now was the thought that there are degrees of aliveness and deadness. We see that in ourselves. We certainly see it in the near-corpses who are our political rulers. Theo had known since the Syntagma taverna that his parents were not dead. But where were they – and where was he - on the spectrum of aliveness? Could he make them, and could he make himself, any more alive? Any more capable of relationship? Could he make his parents come out of solution and crystallize before him? Could he go into solution himself?

And then there was the matter of his facelessness. Until now it had been merely disconcerting and curious. But it started to matter. He'd got himself back, but that, he now saw, wasn't the end of the story.

He didn't need a face for himself, but without a face how could he relate to his re-found parents? And without relationships, did it mean anything to say that he was himself? Without relationships he soon wouldn't be anything – let alone himself. How could he smile or cry without a face? He recognized them as they came out of the surf, but did they know him? It is a terrible thing not to be able to show that you love or hate or indeed that *you* are at all.

The deadest thing in the world is a waterlogged feather in February: one of the sinking ones: all its oil long gone into thousands of rainbow mirrors, continents apart: the hooks holding the barbules together gone limp; the quill chamber flooded; the white that used to turn blue over the Laconian Gulf now forever grey. Here is the real triumph of chaos and the dark. And everything knows it. Even the things with disgusting appetites. The feather is a leper. Nothing crawls over it. There are no diatoms in Brownian motion in the quill chambers. It doesn't swish in the water. The water molecules stand aside to let it drift pass. Nothing can bear to touch it in case it is still contagious. The air, for which it existed, has thrown it up. Theo, looking at a February feather, knew that his parents were far less dead than that. That helped him to calibrate his scale of deadness.

All this is exhausting to write, and perhaps to read. It was, believe me, even more exhausting for Theo to live it.

Carrion Crow

The crow knew that Theo was exhausted. She had a keen intuition for exhausted animals. Normally she ate them.

But though the man smelt of collapse, he wasn't for eating. It was interesting. For a crow, that kind of interest is close to affection. That's not to say that real affection was impossible. Anything that clings as tightly to life as that crow can learn to cling also to another creature, and when it does, the clinging is emotional.

The Author

Theo came out of the water after the dolphin-nudging and went straight to the bar.

It was either exactly the right or exactly the wrong time for him to be there. For there had just arrived, in search of orange juice and soul-scalps, a contingent of young, bushy-tailed evangelicals from the caravan park. They bristled with proof texts. Their elastic-waisted trousers bulged with Bible study notes and suppressed libido. Their smiles were as broad as their philosophy was narrow. They despised this world to inherit the next.

Theo looked alone and vulnerable, sitting there at the corner of the bar with his little glass. In their lexicon, to be alone was to be needy, and to be needy was to be in need of Jesus. Or, to be more exact, of a white, kite-surfing metaphor-phobe with immaculate bridge-work and a conviction that the devil's main work is nuance. All young evangelical leaders in this part of the world kite-surfed, so as to be more like the Lord. Didn't He walk on the water? If you did it well you remained unspotted by the sea.

They nestled round him, cocooning him in unconditional love and nylon. Lisa, their public face (and a pretty face it was too) asked him where he was from – which he confirmed was a very good question – and what he thought of the West Country – which he confirmed was a very complex one. She was keen to know if he ever went to church, and was more worried than reassured when he said that he went all the time. Did he, enquired Lisa, have a personal relationship with God? 'Don't we all?' he replied mildly, and they smelt blood.

Being children of the capitalist west, their pitch was straightforwardly consumerist – directed at his self-interest. They assured him that God loved him personally, nodding energetically when he pointed out that this presumably meant that God had a personality.

'His personality', breathed Lisa, '*is* personal love.'

'Even for the caterpillar eaten from the inside by Ichneumon larvae?'[45] asked Theo, genuinely seeking clarification.

'Yes, even for that', beamed Lisa, wondering what on earth he was on about. 'And He sent His Son' (the capitals hissed acidically through the orange juice) 'to Die in Your Place so that You might be Spared. All you have to do is Accept the Free Gift'.

Theo uncurled with the gentleness possible only in a very violent man. Where should he start? And having asked himself that, it was plain that he shouldn't. He should only end. And so, copying Lisa's smile, he said, almost inaudibly, and wholly apologetically: 'It won't do, you know. It's not just *my* life I'm concerned about: it's everyone and everything else's. I don't know what it means to speak of *my* life without speaking too of the lives of all the other creatures who make me what I am. If they die: so do I. I just evaporate. And so unless the death that ate my father and mother can itself be eaten, we're all eaten.'

And as he said this he realized, to his horror and amusement, that he was articulating not only the sort of communitarianism he'd thought he hated in Tolstoy and Marx, but also the notion of *Christus Victor* that had long been the orthodoxy in Orthodoxy.

Whatever its theological merits, it made the evangelicals drink up and bolt for the cover of their caravans and their cognitive dissonance, and so it must be a good thing.

ѰѰѰ

The sea had snored gently for a while. Towards the end of February it rolled over, snorted, and began to heave and blow. It swung like a cradle at first. And then, over an hour, between two and three in the morning, it cut itself free from all domestic simile and was only its awful self; like nothing else.

The razorbills hid in the corners of the wave-alleys; young gulls were smashed; older gulls chewed; a gannet the size of a goose was slammed against a chimney and slithered down the wall, part paté.

If the eel had had shoulders she would have shrugged them. Broken things – food things - sometimes still floundering – rained down onto its head. Imagine your sky pouring with steak and chips.

An arm of an old beech tree shattered the Evangelicals' windscreen. They took it as a demonic act, and were encouraged by the endorsement: only truly faithful warriors of God would be singled out for such malevolent attention.

The crow crouched next to a squirrel in a tree hole. Resin dripped down and stuck them together.

Theo, drenched, ran gleefully up and down the foreshore.

The purest hatred he had ever felt was for the holiday-makers who had sidled into the summer sea with their hands in the figurative pockets of their Speedos. He had begun by thinking it was sacrilegious. But in a way you couldn't blame them, for at these times the sea had withdrawn completely: it simply wasn't the sea.

The hatred, then, was really for their stupid mistake in thinking that they were in the sea. He wanted them smashed for their own good: to teach them a lesson. It wasn't good for them to make a mistake as big or as repercussive as thinking that the absence of the sea was the sea. And he was angry at the sea for withdrawing like this: for making the mistake possible. His desire to see it surge up and be its smashing self was a *moral* desire – like wanting a good God to vindicate himself by avenging wickedness or stopping suffering.

And here it was! Being itself! Mast-snapping, Speedo-shredding, skin-stripping, joint-ripping; scouring, paring, excoriating, polishing, and dividing souls from bodies and bodies from themselves. You are bounteous, but not generous, he heard himself intoning: you grind and get back as powder, in a colloidal suspension, what you gave as a whorl or a striated shell.

It never occurred to him that he might be singing a hymn to Ichneumon larvae.

Dolphin

The dolphin, not liking sea-sickness, was either very deep, where there was different weather, or on the surface, tasting diesel in the thrashed foam, half-remembering that his ancestors had legs.

Coming close to the shore, he raised himself upright and looked at the surging trees, thinking that it would be fun to swim in waves like those.

He saw Theo dancing on the beach. It confirmed his suspicions. This, he thought, was a very ill man. He had seen a cod dance like that when it had a parasitic worm in its brain.

If only the man had taken notice when he had tried to tell him about the bullet. It might all have been different. He had two pictures: of the man lying still on the beach, covered in crabs. And of the man walking on his hind legs in that strange, leaning, unsteady way that humans have. He had a distinct preference for the second picture, but did not reflect on the preference.

The Author

First of all there was water. At the end there will be water. You can go quietly with those facts, or you can struggle.

For the Hebrews, though the spirit of God hovered over the face of the waters, He didn't, for a while, seem to penetrate far beneath the surface. In the sea lived unchained things that challenged the rule of God. The most spectacular miracles of the Hebrew Bible involve God showing that he has jurisdiction over the water. He used the Flood to kill almost everything on earth,[46] he turned the Nile to blood,[47] and the Red Sea was his weapon for annihilating Pharaoh's army.[48] When Jesus walked on the water and subdued the waves, it was a claim to divinity no Jew could miss.[49] After his resurrection he cooked and ate kippers on the beach. Then there's baptism: to press water into service in baptism is to reclaim sovereignty over Leviathan. This divinized water makes you immune to the toxic waters of death, through which all must pass. But ordinary water remained deadly. Wine is what happens (at least at weddings) when divinity gets properly to work on water.[50] You shouldn't mess with the original stuff. It's all right to eat land animals, and to eat fish (particularly when you've been dead for three days) is a sign that you're on the right side - that Leviathan can be burgled.

But note God's disapproval (actually his *disowning*) of the creatures that try to be at home both on earth and in the water. He created the sea creatures and the land creatures. But the amphibians? They're not mentioned.[51] And they're certainly not kosher. They're good for plagues but not for dinner.

Perhaps Theo, like frogs, was trying to have it both ways. Living on the edge of the sea like that. Perhaps that's why he was so wretched. He was both inedible (for clean people) and incapable of enjoying his food.

Rachel

One day some people came into the pub. Dad was there and so was Theo. The people started talking to Theo. They seemed really interested in him but they didn't seem interested in Dad. I don't blame them. Dad is very boring.

They were asking Theo lots of questions about stuff. One of the ladies used to be Theo's girlfriend. He called her Sarah and they looked at each other in a really weird way. He didn't seem to mind the questions much, but didn't give them very long answers. I would have got into trouble if I had talked like that.

Then they started talking about Jesus and Theo started laughing. That was very rude. Some man put his hand on Theo's shoulder and closed his eyes and started saying something and then Theo said that he should get a life and the man said that he had one and that he was trying to make sure that Theo had one too. And then the man and the ladies went away and left some crisps behind which I ate. Sarah gave Theo some sort of note on the back of a ticket. He put it into his pocket quickly. And then Theo burped and bought an egg from a jar which looked like something in a museum. He ate it and felt ill and went back to his house which he calls his shell or something like that. Then we went home and watched a programme about a man with a bad leg.

Theo

Ah, the dolphin's back. What can be done to make it stay away? A big dose of Clozapine, I suspect; or some other potent anti-psychotic.

Yes, I was struggling with bereavement. Most humans are. Yes, my tendency (like that of most overeducated people) is to see my particular distress as a member of a genus of distressing experiences.

Isn't that a good thing? Or would you dismiss it as cowardly evasion? An attempt to evade the particular by dodging into the generic? An attempt to avoid the concrete by coming all over abstract? An attempt to dilute my own misery in the misery of others?

I'd have thought it means I'm less likely to be a sniveling, self-centred whinger, and more likely to empathise with others in a similarly horrible place. It's not obviously contemptible to try to see the wider context: to see myself as unexceptionable; subject to the same forces as everyone else.

On a point of structure: You shouldn't have all that re-visiting, should you? It's clumsy. Back to Sheffield. Back to Greece. It breaks up the flow. Or is it an artfully artless picture of ebbing and flowing? Humans are tides: geddit?

On another point: I'm bemused. Where are you going with this? Shouldn't you make up your mind – for readability if for no other reason – whether nature is benign or malignant, whether God is transcendent or immanent, whether minds are transparent or not, whether mind emerges from matter or is distinct from it or entangled with it? And shouldn't you decide whether this is a treatise on theodicy, a memoir of bereavement, a vaguely maritime prose poem, a hectoring if eclectic religious tract, a Greek nationalist hymn, a wildly dishonest biography, a scrapbook of shamanic ravings, an allusive but incoherent epistemology, a damp Creation myth, flatulent mythopoeia? Or what?

I bet we'll get the Lady of the Lake soon.

The Author

On your last points: how can I make up my mind?

The book is about the sea, and so about everything.

As to re-visiting, I agree, in principle, that re-visiting is poor literary form. No doubt all the 'How to get your novel published' books advise against it. I can see why. But almost all of life involves re-visitings (of places, people, ideas, anxieties, and so on. Dogs return to their vomit because they are dogs: Humans to their pasts because they are humans). So in telling a human story it is rather important to consider all the harking back. That would be true even if you hadn't in fact kept on going back to Sheffield and to Greece. Since you did, I don't have much choice, do I?

Chorus

Why cannot mortals eat gratefully the meal laid before them? Why do they lust for dainties that the gods know will make them sick, and which the gods, in their benevolence, withhold? The ambrosia of the high ones is deadly to men made of dust.

10. The Sun

ΨΨΨΨΨΨΨΨΨΨΨΨΨΨΨΨΨΨΨΨΨΨΨΨΨΨΨΨΨΨΨΨΨΨΨΨΨΨΨΨΨΨΨΨΨΨΨΨ

The Author

It wouldn't have worked if the sword had been thrown into a *wood*. It had to go into water, and be caught by a human hand. It is not clear why this is so.

How are we to imagine the body to which that hand was attached? Was it spongy and rutted with long immersion? Did fish peck at its skin cells? Were there gills in the woman's neck with fronds like bloody feathers – perhaps setting off the dress nicely?

In the Arthurian literature adventures only ever start to happen when the protagonist gets lost. It is hard to get lost on the land. It is hard not to get lost at sea. At night at sea you don't even know which is up and which is down. With that confusion comes the exciting knowledge that it doesn't matter much.

ΨΨΨ

As well as having no face, Theo had holes in his head where memories should have been. He had no detailed memory of specific events. He remembered only that the events had happened. He remembered that he had kissed a woman, but not when, or where, or the colour of her lips. He remembered that he had ridden to the West Country on his bike, but not the route, the weather, or what he'd had in his sandwiches. He was a list of headings. He had a number of statuses (kisser, biker) but those statuses had no content or meaning. He'd always been rather like that: more of a CV than a person.

Sometimes he was rather relieved by this. It gave him a sort of immunity. There may be nothing in me that can be redeemed, he thought, but there's nothing that can be damned either. I don't taste of enough to be a desirable supper for demons. And my faceless-ness? Well, my dad might not recognize me, and I might never be able to show my mum I'm hurting, but I'll never be stuffed and put up on the wall of a billiard-room.

ΨΨΨ

As he walked along the shore he swung his father's olive wood *kom-boloi*. Every bead was striated. Each dark line represented a winter. Warm, wet summers were thick and pale. He had at least five years between his fingers. His father's fingers had always stroked the years.

We think we keep the artifacts of the dead in order to remember them. It is a half truth, like so many thoughts in these shadowlands. We keep the artifacts because the dead are inherent in them. A truc-ulent uncle trembles in an ink well: a mother infuses her chair. Habits cannot be destroyed by fire or burial, and habits crystallize in things and in places, continuing to affect them. The ink goes down. The chair rocks. This isn't a conventional haunting. You might as well say that the ink well haunts the uncle.

Like the sea and like happiness, the dead cannot be approached di-rectly. Try to do so and you'll find something else altogether, and I promise that you won't like it at all. Humans are far too big and good for Ouija boards.

If an inkwell can be inhabited because of its centrality to a habit, the holy dead must be there at the Byzantine liturgy, performed with exactly that intonation and choreography for fifteen hundred years. They drink and eat from the same golden spoon as today's commu-nicants; they kiss the icons on the same spot. The feet of the Virgin in a modern Oxford church are warm from the lips of a repentant eleventh century Ikarian pirate.

If that's true of inkwells, chairs, and paintings (and even if it's not true of any of them) it is true of DNA. Theo's stroll along the tide line was affected by one of his distant uncles - a dead marine mollusc from Tasmania. One edge of his thought was drawn by an old aunt – a Cambrian arthropod; another by a nasty shock a small stooping biped had in Ethiopia five million years ago; yet another by a gene flicked on by a wolf some time in late antiquity and kept on by a generation of Viking rape-threats.

He swung his dead dad round his fingers: clackety clack, clackety clack.

ᛨᛨᛨ

The sun never leaves Greece. Even when there is snow on the olives and frost on the moustaches, the sun is just locked up for a while in the stones. If you kick them hard, summer oozes out in January.

But it had left the shores of the little brown sea, and who can blame it? It hadn't been appreciated by a discriminating audience when it was around. People had sat in it fully clothed, and eaten ice cream and chips in it, and drunk cold chemicals in it, and closed the blinds so that it wouldn't interfere with their view of their screens. The migration routes and calendars of birds and butterflies are changing, and perhaps one day the sun too will decide not to come north.

For the moment, though, the sun persisted in its habit of migration, and so the days started to stretch. At first there was no audible creak; but then, if you were a careful, attentive earwig, you *could* hear noises. The earth's skin and the sea's skin were stiff drum-heads. Pale things nuzzled through the soil, pushing worms and sand grains and bits of mould aside in their hurry. There was a swishing in the ground; a grating against grit; and, when the things got to the edge of the skin, a pushing, a tenting, and a pop as they became self-bursting pimples. The dead were spun, shoved and raised.

Inside some of the birds that picked along the sea-fringe and bobbed and bustled in the surf, ovaries swelled, pressing, irritating, and quickening the colon. Just as in humans, travel and sex meant butterflies in the tummy. The little brown sea became drab, its fish sour, its cockles metallic.

The birds smelt the road that farted along the shore, and compared it with the trackless beaches of the north. They thought of the brown sea, foaming with soap and navigated by flotillas of turds, and of another sea of high blue and white, swaying with silver; of shiny black backs puffing and sputtering. These pictures were abstractions with clear emotional colour. Call it preference rather than emotion if it helps you to relax and not throw the book down with a snort. The birds' brains (neurological hardware, if you must) flicked between the pictures, comparing and calculating. And then, the calculation complete and the commitment absolute, they emptied their cloacas one final time, pattered across the water for take-off or pushed into the air so that the wind could catch them, locked onto the poles and the stars, climbed above the flurry of the sea, and headed for the promise.

ΨΨΨ

In the sea, blocks of water levered each other up and pushed each other down. Fish, shrimps, and plankton lurched inside their blocks. Fish in one block passed fish in another, going in different directions – as if they were in adjacent lifts in an office building. They all wanted to go up now, for though there was heat deep down, there was more light every day at the surface, and they knew that light meant life in a way that heat did not. They wanted to live. This was *will* in action, just as much as a well-considered marriage proposal, and far more than most political decisions. But going up wasn't so simple.

It is a mistake to think of the sea as soup. Diffusion is an overrated force. Better to think of the sea as a shifting conglomeration of city states. The sea's borders slowly change – though there are mountain ranges that make some borders hard. Alliances are painfully rene-gotiated. But the sun puts the negotiators in a good mood. It melts borders. When the sun comes back there's more commerce between the deep and the shallow, the north and the south. And indeed be-tween humans and non-humans. I do not know why. Perhaps every-thing worships the sun and everything feels that it is proper to smile at other members of the congregation.

Since autumn the mackerel had hung like motes at the very edge of the deep sea, living on the memory of last summer frozen in oil. As winter wore on, the bellies of the females grew tense and heavy with eggs, and they squeezed gas into their swim bladders to stay where they were. No sun came down to them, but they knew from the creak of the water that it had arrived, and over weeks their noses started to tilt up toward it. Then there was a quiver in the tail of an old male at the centre of the shoal. The next day it was copied by two old ladies. And suddenly it became a thrust from them all. The shoal pushed up into the light.

Theo had given up his twice-daily bobbing. He now swam several times a day. He had become inflexibly and liberatingly ritualistic in the sea. He had to submerge his head five times: ten if it was cold enough to hurt. He had to draw water into his mouth so that the suspended sand rasped his tongue. He had to salute an old bass in a cul-de-sac off a kelp glade, whose gill plate could slice through a pudding spoon. He had to pass through an arcade of razors and be thrown by a wave over the rail of a lobster boat whose captain was still down there somewhere. He had to touch a constellation of limpets in the pattern of Orion, and swim back shorewards through an undersea rock arch. When he came out, he came out backwards, always facing the sea; backing away like the Hasidim in their silk coats leaving the Western Wall.

Having done this, he was freer on land than he had ever been. The rock arch was the door to something new, but he could not go far beyond the threshold.

Clam

It was barely spring for the clams of the Severn Sea. Oestrogens from the urine of the south-west's self-sterilizing women, squirted into the ocean from sewage works, had turned clam testes into hybrid ovotestes.[52] Ovotestes did not know how to respond to the rising sun. These clams were graphs more than minds, but the graphs were flat, and they flattened the graphs of everything round them. The sap rose less in the wood. The crow's eye was duller. Petals were not so shiny. The dolphins did not jump so high.

Dolphin

Though his sense of distance and shape came mainly through the sounds that clicked through his jaw, his forehead, and the sea, the dolphin had not been gone from the land so long – nor were his moods so tethered to the burst of fish between his teeth – that the seasons meant nothing. He idled in the winter: enduring, treading water with feet that hadn't been there for forty million years, listening to his heart, rising to the surface in the hope of sun, sinking like a roller blind when he found only the cold dark.

He tried to turn the dark into a virtue, diving two hundred metres to the shell of a battleship, where he bent and snapped a long, old fish untidily, as a child snaps a green twig, and as a child's own rubbery bones are snapped.

Then he overreached himself. Boredom and borderline depression did it.

The battleship, to a battered psyche, was a game; its hard lines a bracing change from the curves of the sea. An old octopus was at the helm. Its arms waved around the wheel – a semi-brain in each of them; each arm a semi-autonomous province; consciousness delegated to each by the central bundle of neurones where, if you were a naïve Cartesian who knew nothing of biology, you'd think its self was concentrated.[53]

There was a porthole from which a Danish sailor, desperate to see his daughter, had pushed in hope and horror, leaving a fringe of skin and hair which had been trimmed by the bony jaws of big-eyed fish. The dolphin squeezed through. He was now in a metal box.

This was bad. It was not just that the dolphin (a wild thing, whose place was the whole world), was confined like a Bedouin herder in an air-conditioned office. That would have been bad enough. But there is a particularly horrible sort of claustrophobia that happens when you are an echo-locating animal in an enclosed space. Your clicks go out in all directions. These clicks are designed to probe long distances through salt water to the yielding bodies of fish. When you are in a small metal box your clicks bounce hard and almost immediately back to you from all around. And not just that: the pulses ricochet around: you get a frantic, undecodable mess of information; information that has crossed other information and become contaminated and useless. A click from a bolt in a ceiling hatch glances off a floor screw and gets trapped in a corner before going back to your jaw. It's like being on the internet. Evaluation is impossible. When there is too much information, nothing works.

Then there was the physical pain. The storm of amplified noise hurt, as it hurts to stand next to big speakers at a club. And an aesthetic disgust like that felt by a gentle folk musician, in corduroy trousers, used to lilting songs and clairvoyant relationships with the other musicians, standing next to those speakers. The dolphin was revolted by the contrast between the subtlety of its usual perception (it could taste moods and minute gradations of density) and the clang grind scratch scrape of the box. Revulsion implies a love of whatever is opposed to the revolting thing, and it was love and lust of subtlety and distance that now made the dolphin frantic.

A dolphin trembles all over when pressed lightly with a human finger. As the dolphin lunged forward his head hit the rusty steel about a hundred thousand times harder than that finger pressure. The only comparable experience in the life of a normal dolphin is right at the end, when the teeth of a killer whale meet in its throat.

If he could have panted he would have done. The shock, disgust, fear, and pain cost him a lot of oxygen. His chest was tight. Soon he would have to breathe the mud-salt-fumes of Wales. So he collected himself (just think what that entails), stopped his click-shrieks, and instead sent small gobbets of sound into the dark.

One of them never returned. That meant, the dolphin concluded, that it had gone through the porthole.

Though the situation was desperate, there was time for relief; for thoughts of green and blue and, most of all, of family and friends; of bodies alongside one another; of stroking flippers; of the thrill of normality known only to the condemned.

But in fact the sound had found two holes, not one. The first was big – big enough for the dolphin. The second was the size of a fist.

The dolphin pushed himself through the first, which led out onto the bridge. He expected to swim straight ahead and out, but there was no escape. He spat out sound, and the sounds rattled back around his head; a hail of acoustic shrapnel; bouncing, criss-crossing, weaving a net of sound in which he was caught.

The octopus was also in the net, and didn't like it.

One of its arms – one of its departments – slapped the dolphin's face. Neither the octopus's central brain or that brain's local franchise in the fluttering silk-iron limb knew immediately what it had hit, but it held on. Indeed it barely had a choice – any more than the sucker of a child's play arrow has a choice whether to hold or release a wet window. For the sucker was on the dolphin's eye.

At this point physics took over:

Let x = the retractive force of the ocular muscles, the optic nerve, and various pieces of connective tissue.

Let y = the force required to detach the sucker from the surface of the eye.

Let z = the force exerted on the eye by the pull of the octopus arm and the attempt of the dolphin to wrench himself free.

Provided that $y > z$, then, if $z > x$, the dolphin's eye leaves the socket.

The provisos were satisfied, and the eye did.

If you doubt the importance of situation and context, look at an eye that's dangling out.

Are there, I wonder, any situations in Theo's life in which physics rules quite so simply?

ᛉᛉᛉ

Nausea works rather differently in dolphins than in us. It doesn't rise from the belly, but is felt as a tightening in the temples. It flashes on and off in red and gold, and settles into red waves.

Another eye has been lost in this book, of course. The gull lost an eye to the crow's beak. But that did not involve any loss of self – just loss of part of the world in which the self was embedded. The gull's self could be, and was, quickly relocated. With the dolphin it was different. The boundary between him and the world he had lost was not as clearly drawn as in the gull. To lose the perception of one side was to destroy a big part of himself. It was a bereavement.

Human eyes, since they look forward, are more or less interchangeable. There is little sensory change when we lose a single eye. And no ontological change: our worlds are so virtual – so self-created – that they have little relationship to the objective realities of the external world. But dolphins live, as we do not, in the real world. A one-eyed dolphin might as well have a wholly new name.

So we have a one-eyed gull and a one-eyed dolphin. It would be cute, wouldn't it, if the gull became the dolphin's left side and the dolphin became the gull's right side? Sorry: it didn't happen. There are all sorts of reasons why not: some of them very obvious.

The new dolphin smashed through the cabin roof into the see-sawing sea, and smashed through the water too, eye trailing like a pompom, up and up and into the air.

It took a week for the eye to detach. It bobbed along on the surface for a while, and then slid to the sea floor, where it was gathered by a crab with long maternal arms, and hugged, and nibbled.

Don't you dare think that the crab is beneath you. It has barely changed since the Jurassic. You have just arrived. The fact that it hasn't changed much in a couple of hundred million years means that it was superbly refined *then*. You're still learning how to use your mere two bald legs, and not making a great job of it. If there are any grounds for chronological snobbery, they're all on the crab's side.

Carrion Crow

The crow left the land during the winter days, returning to the wood only to sleep. Winter didn't come to the shore as sharply as it came to the fields and the trees. Since December she had picked stabbingly through rock pools like a psychopathic old woman through a jumble sale.

She knew that the sea did not end where the exposed sand began. It is hard to know where it did begin or end. Perhaps it went all the way under the hills to London. Marine worms swam through the damp sand. The crow felt the rasp of their bristles against quartz boulders. The vibration shook the scales of her feet: enough to infuriate but not enough to locate.

Anything from the sea seemed fair game. The crow had never seen the man spare anything from the sea, and it was clear enough that the sea wouldn't care about anything in it being killed. But the crow had seen the man gather up a trembling mouse in his hand, blow on it to make it warm, and put it gently at the foot of a wall.

The crow imitated actions, sounds and habits. And so when a shrew came out of the field one bitter day, when frost had sealed all the worms into the ground, she looked at it and decided for a moment not to kill.

After the decision came a wondering at herself, and a wondering at the shrew. It was strange that the shrew was alive at all. It had to eat – by killing - six hundred times a day: that's once every two and a half minutes, around the clock. Its heart did not beat but hummed. Its weight had dropped by a fifth, its skull and its liver had shrunk, and the crow knew something of its terrible precariousness and defiance.

It didn't do any good. The crow was too cold. The bones of the shrew were in the next pellet but one.

Yet the taste of that momentary restraint was delicious. The crow
never forgot it. And, who knows? Perhaps amongst the squeals and
peristaltic gurgles there was the click of a genetic switch. Remember
that Lamarck is back, prowling the beaches and flapping through
the woods.[54] It's not ridiculous to think that he might have taught a
bit of kindness.

The Author

One March morning, having swum through the arch and backed
away from the sea, Theo bent and looked into a pool of sea water.
He could see part of his face! It was faint, but there was no doubt
about it. He touched it, and could feel it too.

He ran back into the sea and scrubbed his face with seaweed, expecting the face to come off. It didn't. The pool told him that there
was more of it than ever. He scrubbed again, and this time all of
him looked back at him.

He dressed quickly, crossed himself for no reason he could explain,
and ran up onto the cliffs and along the path that followed the coast
westward.

At the cliff edge, hanging out into the air, swaying in the hot fishy
breath of gulls, shiny with the scales and papery with the swim bladders of herring, crusty with the pocked skin of dabs and slithering
things without names, were hazel, oak, ash, sycamore and beech, all
thin and hunched against the wind. Beneath them were Dog's mer-
cury, and Coke cans and wild privet and grand papers full of lies,
and ivy, and little local papers full of kindnesses, courage and despair, and honeysuckle, and a poisoned goose with a liver the size
of a walnut, and black bryony, and a video game that had lasted long
enough to trash someone's childhood, and stinking iris, and a hat

bought for a wedding and never worn, and Hart's tongue, and a beaker of Roman glass, and Spurge laurel, and a hand saw with the blade twisted to one side because it was used for half a century by someone whose shoulder went for a wander through his chest one afternoon at Arras.

Theo chanted the names of the plants as he walked – names he had not known he knew. There was power in the names. Because many had used them – especially when stroking the petals – there was now a real concordance between the names and what the plants were. A similar thing had happened to Theo: because he had been called Theo he had become Theo, and could not now be accurately called Tom. His face grew and solidified in the sun. Tom became less plausible with each flower, step and photon.

Theo might have come across so far as coldly ungrateful. He was not. It was just that the things that most demanded gratitude were sacred to him, and thus undiscussable and unthankable. It is hard to address personal thanks to a sacred *principle* or a holy *force*. But now, and suddenly, beneath his feet and spurting out of the earth, were things that plainly demanded gratitude and which, he had just discovered, had names by which they could be addressed: names in which they could be thanked. They were more – not less - themselves because they had names, and so the thanks could be more fulsome and more accurately directed.

Floodgates opened, never to shut again. At first the gratitude was only for vegetative things; the grass of the cliff; green spikes; veins full of last autumn's sun; tree-skin peeling in silver ringlets; crocuses that ejaculated golden sperm onto his shoes as he brushed them; austere black twig-tracery. But then the category of gratitude-deserving things widened; the rockery in his childhood garden; a guinea-pig; the guinea-pig's hutch; the hands that had made the hutch; the womb that had incubated the hands. Or perhaps all these things were vegetative. He was never sure. But, whatever the right analysis, he had a jolly walk along the cliff top, smiling with the ancient folly of the wise, and bought himself an unseasonal ice cream.

The girl watched him as he licked it, and wondered, between Bible verses, whether she'd lost him for ever, or whether the Lord of Hosts might deign to deliver him again into her hand.

The Lord is a jealous God, and He won't share anyone at all.

Rachel

Theo seemed even more weird than usual. He laughed when there was nothing funny. He drank loads of cider from a little glass and tried to balance the glass on his nose. He bought loads of stuff for people he didn't know, and hit people on the back. That was supposed to be friendly I think. He asked me if I believed in fairies and I said yes and he said quite right. Then he asked if I believed in money and I said yes because I've got some and he said 'Ah, but have you? Or has it got you?' and he laughed again and it really creeped me out. Though he was laughing he wanted to make everything serious. It was a bit like my dad, but worse because I can tell my dad to shut up and he usually does, but you can't tell strangers to shut up, even if they are not really strangers.

He always had a flower in his pocket and he tried to give me one but I said that my dad had said I shouldn't take things from strangers and he thought that was funny.

One day he started to cry. I don't know why. It was SO embarrassing. He showed me some beads and said that they were his dad's and I said that he should give them back to his dad and he said he would.

He said he used to have a girlfriend with hoofs and a tail. That was cool anyway.

I think he still lived by the sea because he had scales on his boots.

Dolphin

Another dolphin – a young, patient female - became our dolphin's left side, attached to him like a remora; shuddering the left world into his flank.

When Theo went in to swim that March morning the young dolphin reported back to the older dolphin's shoulder and belly in a ripple of gentle depolarizations: 'He's fine. He's through the arch. Don't worry.'

The Author

He put his new face to good use. It was stiff at first, but he soon learned to use it for the long-deferred smiling and laughing and crying with his mum and dad.

Immortality, he found, was not the anaemic business of recollection and persisting influence; of commemoration and commiseration; of wraiths at the corner of your eye on a winter afternoon. It wasn't like a bibliographical reference, cited in subsequent generations of articles. It wasn't even about the mere survival of personality.

Survival is a desperate, pathetic word. Immortality was about realization. The resurrection body of Jesus had walked straight through doors and walls. It was *more* material than mud bricks and wood, not less. His dad was bigger and harder than ever. His mother hugged more embracingly than she ever had, and cooked better. They should be up there on the church wall alongside Yiannis the Evangelist and St. Dionysus, their black hair framed by gold-leaf haloes. Poor old John Brown's body might be mouldering in his grave while his soul went marching on, but that certainly wasn't true of anyone called Spyros or Angeliki.

Wine was indeed the blood of God, and his mother and father must be invited each night to the dinner they were at anyway. And since his own body was eternal, and getting more solid all the time, he should feed it and make it dance. Which is precisely what he did, down on his beach that night, though it was March and raining.

ΨΨΨ

Names had been rehabilitated by the cliff-top plants, and, slowly, language, argument and structure were too. He could be a philosopher again. No: he could be a philosopher for the first time. So the handless plants handed Theo back the whole of his academic past. Apollo wasn't apolline without Dionysus. So Theo read Spinoza as he drank Farmer Burt's home brew, skipping merrily between syllogisms and giggling before he vomited over a visiting cat.

ΨΨΨ

It's quite something to get back your face, have a plant approve of your career and for your dead mum and dad to be back home, roasting potatoes, mopping the table, and muttering about the weather and the bloody Turks. It had to be marked. The obvious way was to have a party in the pub. Theo set a date.

Gannet

A gannet came down to the little brown sea from a piece of rock in the Atlantic. Her feathers were too white for the Severn mud. She was a different order of being. When she folded her wings and dived, no mud stained her back. Even when there was no sun in the sky or the sea, there was always some sun trapped in her feathers.

She was thirty-five years old. She knew the fairground rockings and upwellings of Biscay; the killing to be had off Finisterre. She had gagged on a hairy fish with dinner-plate eyes somewhere near Faro, and speared a colostomy bag nowhere near Gibraltar. Her eyes had been grazed by grit streaming out of Mauritania; she had smelt sumptuous fruity decay from the Gambia. Her tongue, sharp as her beak, had curled like a bull-hide whip round the body of the last surviving member of a species of pilchard whose fossils you can see in the Smithsonian.

Now she flapped lugubriously between grid references, staring down beneath the twitching hide of the sea. Yet for the bird this was not 'the sea'. There was nothing chartless or generic about it. It was a mosaic of very different places, each with a centre, a territory, a set of challenges, and a taste.

Seabirds are long-lived because the negotiation of such complex landscapes takes a lot of learning. We too are long-lived. But, these days, our longevity is wasted on us. We don't need to live so long. Our landscapes are typically simple to the point of banality. We can understand them in minutes. Think of the map of Manhattan.

It is very strange that big-brained animals with a taste for pleasure trade lush complexity for arid simplicity. It's all of a piece with every other characteristic of the world of the post-Enlightenment (there's an ironic word!). We take a creature made in the image of God and make it work in a call centre. However fundamentalist your understanding of prayer, God really doesn't work in a call centre. Call centres are blasphemous.

If that's too strong or emetically theological, try this: we take a creature who, if blinded, can teach itself to navigate by echolocation while riding a bicycle through moving traffic,[55] expect it to be satisfied and entertained with 'Britain's Got Talent', and are surprised when it's not. How dumb is that?

The gannet, as she moved between the marine equivalents of a

Malaysian rain forest and a Mongolian steppe, saw Theo pulling himself through the kelp, watched by two conjoined dolphins, and thought that the world it was a-changing – as perhaps it was.

Theo

It is now clear enough what sort of book this is. It is a book of reactionary sermons, which must have been cathartic to preach. I agree with some of them, but I feel used. It is not decent to hijack someone's larynx as you have done. Some is beyond parody: cod psychologizing of me, and actual psychologizing of cod.

It is plain, too, that I am a mere irritant. I doubt you want a response from me. Marionettes don't answer back. But I don't want to roll over.

I'm not, or at least wasn't a whole person, you imply, because of the holes in my memory. That would mean that there are an awful lot of un-whole people – or perhaps you'd call them non-persons – who are nonetheless biologically human. That's a bit of a worry, isn't it? What do you think you can do to these *untermenschen*? But let's not go there. Let's assume I'm the only one who can't connect with an unbroken thread of memory all the events in my life.

What has recall got to do with identity? We don't say that we are un-people because we don't recall our births. Doesn't the fact of consistent behaviour or personality convince you of a consistently present identity? Surely it doesn't matter that I am not my own witness to that consistency? I can call lots of people to say that I am consistently bastardish, and bastardish in a wholly consistent way. The facts of my bastardish behaviour denote at least some degree of agency. And agency denotes identity. Ergo I exist and existed, even though I have no memory of existing.

Isn't this book supposed to be about *me?* As the author, don't you have a problem if there turns out to be no *me* at all? But I can reassure you. Today the thing I call 'I' sat at the edge of the sea with 'my' legs crossed. After a while 'I' noted that 'my' legs hurt. The use of these personal pronouns of course begs the question of whether there is a Theo to whom they relate. But the fact that 'I' can wonder who this 'I' is whose legs hurt suggests strongly that there's an I: *I* doubt, therefore *I* am. So I exist, and your book is saved. A bit of gratitude would be nice.

I got up, stiff-legged. *I* walked along the beach, took off *my* clothes and dived in next to a gull that was not me. This was not a question of my soul commanding my instrumental body to do something. *I* was both of those things at once. Then both of those things put their face into the boiling surf and were hurled back, screaming with the wonder of it all. Then *I* came out, shat tumultuously, and was a confident *agent* for the rest of the day, owing personal duties, having personal preferences, knowing where *I* was and where *I* stopped.

I don't like ice-cream. Never have.

'The girl', I'm told, is in some secure rehab facility in Plymouth, not touring the south west with a group of predatory evangelists.

But it is true that I cross myself, and true that I don't know why, and true that I feel better now, and true that personality seems to be far more robust than any other substance: it is unlikely to be destroyed by fire or sword or larvae. And, yes, there are now two dolphins in the bay by the hut - though you might have spared us that wholly gratuitous fantasy scene about the octopus, which doesn't mesh at all with the story.

Yes, a single gannet has arrived and works its beat like an old-fashioned bobbie.

It took ages to clean the cat.

The Author

There is no secure rehab facility in Plymouth.

The octopus and the dolphin's eye? Gratuitous and off-plot? Yes, this is a book about you. But isn't everything about you? And isn't everything about everything and about everyone? Surely you'd agree, at least in principle? But in fact there's a more obvious reason for including the story. I expect you can work it out.

It's quite something to be convinced by an early morning dip and a crap that the entire world view of the eastern religions is simply wrong. But well done you: it must have been quite a crap.

Chorus

With their faces as well as their hands men show rightful thanks to the immortals. Lips are in the face, and the same words may be spoken with curled or deceitful or truthful lips.

Here too should be an ending, with the man doing what men do, and the gods doing what gods do.

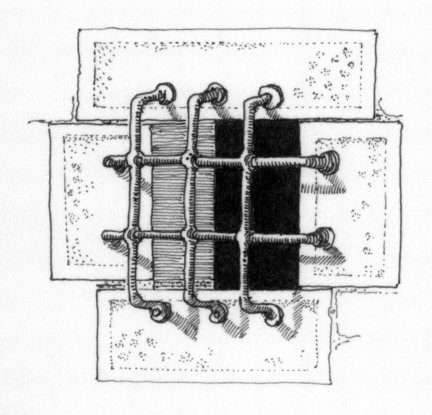

11. The Party

The Author

It all started so well. Theo was in expansive mood. If you didn't know him you'd think him affected beyond belief.

'Welcome, welcome', he boomed to a group of visiting golfers. 'Think about this. You put grapes in a jar and wait, and then in the jar there's something that will turn you into a god for a night. No wonder that God, when he strode through Palestine and the pine woods of Attica, commanded that he be remembered in wine. So let's obey!'

And he poured and poured, and the golfers looked at each other and shrugged, and held out their glasses, and the pub filled up, and still he poured. Then someone came with a dog which could do somersaults, and someone else came with an accordion and started to sing songs about hangmen, and about women who dressed up as men to follow their lovers to sea, and about shortening sail on Magellan Strait and falling from the topsail yard and being eaten by sharks, and then a seagull that had been drinking beer left out for the dog floundered in and stood swaying on the bar.

A farmer pinned his own ear to the bar with a dart. Seconds later it caused admiring applause in Tokyo kitchens and horrified gasps in New Jersey malls.

The gull croaked and went to sleep on a bag of biltong. Fiddlers arrived, and the cadences lurched from major to minor and back, just as they do in real life, and some women tried to dance, but it didn't really work.

A cloud from Cuba dumped an inch of rain and some tropical spiders on the pavement, and everyone apart from the golfers filed out to stand in the rain and filed back in to steam like kettles.

A boat landed. Baskets of fish and lobsters were hauled up to the pub and auctioned for anything but money: hours of plumbing: logs: hundredweights of manure: a Ukrainian meal for four: a stuffed stoat: a strippergram (not Tuesdays, because he had to take the kids to Brownies then): advice on the solution of partial differential equations: the Law Reports (Queen's Bench Division), 1956-2012: herbal tinctures for herpes: a spoon carved from the femur of a mediaeval saint.

An escaped lobster crushed a golfer's testicle. The gull woke up. It poured outside and it poured inside. It was all splendid.

Chorus

And one of the immortals, piqued, bored and mischievous, chose to play – as was her right.

The Author

An old, high-coloured Tory churchwarden who spent his holidays on package tours to Israel elbowed his way through the crowd to Theo.

'You're a philosopher, I hear?'

'Aren't we all? Can I top you up?'

'I want your view. We need to get back to basics, don't we? And that means getting back to the ancient religions, doesn't it? They got it right, those Jews, didn't they?'

Theo's reply was supernaturally gracious.

'But Judaism's not an ancient religion at all', he said. 'It's a fairly recent reaction to empire: to power. It's always been a protest religion – telling the great kingdoms that they're not great at all, and that totalitarianism is doomed.[56]

This beer's not bad at all. They make it in a cowshed up the road. They put bog myrtle in it.

Abraham turned his back on cosmopolitan Mesopotamia and shuffled to a sandy bit of nowhere, Moses gave the finger to mighty Egypt, and the Hebrews found their way out of the Babylonian net and back to Jerusalem, which was a ruin.

Or perhaps you'd like a dose of this? Steve makes it from potato peelings.

And ever since, if we draw a polite veil over recent Israeli politics, the Jews, with apparent powerlessness, have continued to insist on their own difference from the zeitgeist; mocking the zeitgeist, often in poems shrewdly too clever to be decoded. The powers that patronized or persecuted them have all fallen. The Jews remain. Jews are always at the barricades. They don't burn incense in the Temple any more, but instead, when they're being really Jewish, they burn tyres at barricades.

Drink up. Drink up. You must drink up. And have a slice of Mrs. Jenkins' roadkill pie.

Christianity is a logical, natural extension of the Jewish protest against Empire. This time it's a protest against the hegemony of death.'

'You know, Theo', drawled a bored Glaswegian tourist. 'I get a hard-on just hearing you talk.' His mate cackled and dug into a bag of crisps.

Theo, almost gently, and with the assurance of millennia, leant forward and, not having a bronze sword to hand, broke their noses.

Herring gull

From the chimney of the chip shop next door the gull looked down with his one eye at the infrared steam rising from the policeman's bald head. His own head was cocked to one side, which made it look wise. There was red, too, invisible to humans, in the flashing blue light, and an alluring smell of sick came from the back of the van.

The Author

Yes, the stale State air in the van smelt of sick all the way along the winding road to Taunton.

ΨΨΨ

There was a court. It examined the forces involved in the smashing of the noses.

'You are not guilty of assault if you have acted reasonably and pro-portionately in defence of yourself or another', Theo's barrister ponderously said. 'I don't really think that helps us here, does it?'

Since the question begged so many questions, and because he had been up all night listening to his cell mate weeping, Theo was too tired to start. So he just smiled, said, 'Probably not', and duly pleaded guilty. He got a discount of a third for that guilty plea, which seemed bizarre to him. Why should a refusal to explore important philo-sophical questions result in a shorter time in prison?

ΨΨΨ

So for a year, in Her Majesty's name, Theo was violated. The sexual violation was merely the most predictable, and so the dreariest. In most respects the violation was no greater than that involved in most types of employment, and the conversation and the morals were better than in any merchant bank or advertising agency. Most of the inmates were gently ironic burglars, colourful, self-mocking fraudsters, or Falstaffian rioters. There was a good library, the food was excellent, and his mum and dad were on good form. Ragwort grew in the exercise yard, exotic lichens on the window sills, and jackdaws clinked metallically on the barbed wire. The greatest privation was the jangle of TV and radio, but there were earplugs.

He had arrived expecting to be refined by degradation. He'd welcomed the idea, thinking that since refinement had to come some time, it might as well come now, with the government picking up the bill, and while he was young enough to benefit from the exercise. So he was rather disappointed that it was all so ordinary: that on his release there would still be work to do.

He thought about killing himself, because it seemed poetically necessary to consider it. For a while he couldn't think of a compelling reason not to do so, and then he came up with two arguments, both of which he thought were rather good. First: Gregory of Nazianzus says that each and every human being contains the entire universe.[57] And, second, human beings are constellations of divine sparks. 'To kill myself is one thing'. He observed to his notebook. 'To annihilate a universe is quite another. Suicide is one thing: Deicide is another.'

So instead of hanging himself from the cell door, he hung on. He learned to pity the strutting presumption of the warders; to laugh at the machine that thought it had crushed him.

Our own assessment of fragility is usually wrong. We think that big machines are robust. They're not. They fall, and fall fast and hard. If you want real strength, think of a storm petrel, which weighs an ounce, has a heart that flutters like a mouse's, and for decades rides storms, from Scotland to South Africa, dancing on the waves, while our ludicrous empires wane and political speeches vanish into the void. It's true that the meek will inherit the earth. Get amongst them if you're wise.

The transition from the wild shore to the cell was nothing. What must it be like for a Manx Shearwater, which inhabits the air in the troughs of Atlantic waves, and travels each year from Wales to Argentina and then back, to blunder every summer night into island bracken and scrabble into a burrow? Our lives have no transition so dramatic other than birth and death.

ΨΨΨ

In prison Theo brushed up his carpentry, read a lot of Kazantzakis, learned Turkish, and did an online marine biology course. He came out thinner and quieter and rented a workshop at the harbourside.

Theo

'Her Majesty's Prison, Pentonville, Barnsbury, London
Dear Sir,
I would be very grateful for your help.
The map on the BTO website of the recoveries of British/Irish ringed gannets shows one recovery in what appears to be western Turkey. The table summarising the recoveries makes no mention of Turkey. Nor is there any mention in the detailed text dealing with the recoveries. The table does refer to 12 birds recovered from the 'Mediterranean' - so possibly the Turkish bird is included in this figure. The relevant map on the Euring site does not show any recoveries from Turkey.

Can you help at all about where and when this Turkish-recovered bird
was found, where and when it was ringed, and any other details?
Many thanks and all best wishes.
Professor Theo Theotakis.'

The British Trust for Ornithology

'Dear Professor Theotakis,
Many thanks for your letter. Your surmise is correct. The bird was
apparently recovered in the 'Gulf of Iskenderun', presumably offshore,
though the circumstances are coded as 'unknown', so it has been
registered as being in the Mediterranean Sea. We only provide details for
countries with fewer than 5 records, and there are obviously more than
this for the Mediterranean as a whole, so it doesn't appear specifically.
The bird was apparently ringed as a chick on the Bass Rock in July
1964. I'm afraid I don't have any more details than that to hand.
I hope that helps.
Yours sincerely.'

The Author

Gannets hit the sea at sixty five miles an hour. Their heads and
chests have permanent air bags to minimize the damage from the
collision. Their nostrils open into their mouths: if they didn't, salt
water would be squirted up into the brain.

Chorus

Now let it work! This was more than the goddess foresaw when she
started the game, but she will now enjoy the spectacle from her seat
on the mountain.

12. The boat

The Author

Theo watched his breath as it poured into and out of his body. 'Who's watching it?' he asked. 'Is the person who watched that breath the same one who watched *that* one? And who's the person who has formed the intention to watch the next one?'

The breath eroded his questions. He sat until the thrill of his own breath matched the trill of the oystercatcher and he didn't know where one stopped and the other began. No one knows much about themselves. That's a worry. Not only does it make us frightened and frightening; it also lays the foundation for further crisis. If we know nothing about ourselves as observers, how can we say anything about what we observe? But Theo had started to know.

The epiphany of the spring plants had shown him the power and glory and terror of words, and he tried hard not to speak. When he spoke it was gentle, but he knew that gentle too was a barn owl's flight over a twilight field, and that gentleness can sometimes be in the service of a swoop. He never went now to the pub. If anyone came out to the hut he answered them softly and gently ushered them away. He had been all words. Now that he knew what words were, he was no words.

He watched the beach.

The sea in coastal waters is elastic. Tides come in like pizza dough under a rolling pin. You roll one bit, and it retracts, and you think you've made no progress. But you have: there's a little less elasticity next time.

He gathered himself, forcing all his bits into one place that he could call him – so that his splendid new face could tell an honest story about what *he* was feeling.

He stayed watching because he had learned that nowhere in the world gives you something for nothing. If you want to understand a river you have to swim in it in all seasons, and sleep by it, if not in it. If you want to understand a moor you'll need to run over it until it hurts, and the more pain and the longer the run, the more the land will give of itself. This shouldn't be a surprise. All relationships are like that.

What is surprising is how local the spirits are who have to be appeased, and how small their jurisdiction. I (for instance) had thought that by suffering in the woods and streams and high places of Exmoor I'd at least have a letter of introduction to the daemons of that little Somerset harbour a few miles east when I moved in there. Not so: I had to start from scratch.

Poseidon seems to have franchised out some minor jurisdiction to lesser, local deities, but the franchise is restricted to knockabout, everyday, inshore business. Even there he retains the right to intervene. I know he's fond of offerings, and quick to stamp on cockiness, but I thought that a lot of seasickness in Orkney, a hell of a scare off Scarborough, and the loss of a finger on the sea ice near the North Pole might have counted for something when I came to the Severn Sea. But no: I had no credit at all.

Theo did, I think. Surely the sea inside his chest next to the bullet, and the leg slashed on the rock, and all those humble backings-out from the waves cannot have gone unnoticed. But this credit with the sea wouldn't buy him much. The sea isn't like the land.

If you run or walk consistently over a piece of land, sweating and bleeding into it, it becomes a part of your body: it begins to throb and shiver with you. That's a great honour, since the land is so much bigger and older than you.

This doesn't work with the sea – though it might work with a stretch of beach. The waves never roll in time to your heart, or subside as you raise a companionable hand. The subduing of the Galilean waves was a far greater display of divinity than any healing.

The sea gives nothing back. Or perhaps it just demands everything before it'll give you anything. It is beyond personality and impersonation, and so beyond caprice, prediction, appeal or mercy. Beyond gender: the great seething He-She. It was, and is, and for our sins is rising up to get us.

But perhaps I'm deluding myself about the kindness and responsiveness of the land. Perhaps running and walking over it bind it companionably to me because over the years I've eroded the equivalent of a grave. Perhaps the moor and the sea really speak the same diabolical language.

Theo

You *are* morbid! You're not dealing well with the idea of extinction, are you?

I wonder if your aversion to death is simply aesthetic? An aesthetic aversion to worms and smells, allied to a conservative fear of change? Which you then philosophise into a creed? Like an Alabama fundamentalist finding buggery aesthetically distasteful, and clutching at a frond of scripture to justify the aversion?

But I'm going back to my old dialectical habits. Sorry. I wish we could talk. Truly I do. I think now that you've tried to see things as they were. Things are different now. I'd like to explain, and I'd like to listen. But we're out of time.

The Author

Guillemots defend the smallest home territory of any bird. Though for two thirds of the year they ride the wild green sea and the corkscrew winds of deep heaven, they come back year after year to the same few square inches of shit-stained cliff. I do not understand this dissonance between wilderness and urbanity. I do not know what it says about the sea.

Nor did Theo, but his ignorance worried him as mine does not worry me.

Thinking about the guillemot's rock-squat took away some of Theo's contempt for the land, but still he gazed out to sea for his salvation. Then, one June night, he came out of the hut as the last light drained into the sea. A cuckoo was calling in one of the coombes running down to the beach. He climbed towards it, crawling the last quarter of a mile up a ditch, with stickyweed clinging to his jacket and nettle weals padding out his nose.

At last, because there is grace and power still in the world, he was under the cuckoo tree. He was so close to the bird that he could hear the air rasp over its larynx in the moment before the 'cuck'.

ΨΨΨ

For Theo, it was all and always about the gods in whom he so devoutly disbelieved. He'd been favoured. Because he got so close to the cuckoo, he was placated for the summer. He wondered about staying. He looked to the land as he had not done since he first arrived.

He walked the lanes and lay still in a field for two nights and a day until a hare walked over his back. He studied the earth under his fingernails and in the claws of a crow strung up on a gate. He mapped the runs of beetles and voles under the grass canopy.

He got to know and name each of the petals on five daisies in front of the hut. He visited them morning and night like a shepherd doing the rounds of the sheep. He knew their folds, their stains, and the angles they made as they ticked open and shut with the mounting and dismounting sun. He was diminished when one fell. Bees feeding on his flowers made him jealously proprietorial.

He paced out his patch. It ended at the tide-line (he wasn't stupid or brave). He lived on roots, rabbits and rainwater from the patch. A rabbit an inch the other side of the border was safe because there had to be rules, and some of the most important rules were very local. He was thirsty for the *particular*. He was disappointed that his own dung smelt so generically human.
With this new-found attachment to land-life, he even thought about earning.

He thought of nature writing, but dismissed it as exploitative: as a sort of farming: using a piece of land to turn a profit. It would have stopped him living in the Pleistocene, and hence from being what he (and everyone else) really was.

He thought about teaching, but he'd have to leave the patch, or have it invaded, and, anyway, there probably wasn't much of a market for teaching that went: 'Don't know. Sorry.'

He thought of selling rabbit skins, but each of the skins was too much itself: a whorl there; a patch of white there. It wasn't respectful to turn them over to someone who wouldn't note the differences.

He gave up the idea of earning.

It was a succulent summer. It dripped sweet gold into his mouth. There was sun on the backs of gulls, and because they ate chips with brown sauce, they didn't kill. In the hot cloisters at the top of the oaks, where light behaved as it does at the bottom of a stream, olive-green birds with hearts the size of peanuts pulled off the ticks they had brought from the Congo and sucked back their own blood through holes in the tick's chest.

A girl on a horse paced every day at tea time through the wood, but never went into the patch. The pub roared with people from the caravan site, but it was too far from his patch for Theo to hear.

The daisies did what they were meant to do, and then collapsed. Owl chicks grew fat and brown on mice of about their own age – mice that did not understand the idea of 'above'. Buzzards got sunburn round their eyes. Flies hatched and stretched, pumping brake fluid into their wings to make them stiff, took their place in a humming mist for an hour, and then folded themselves into the ground or became part of the wind. Swallows' tails whistled as they touched the grass heads, snapping at insects kicked up by the cows. Swifts, faces open like trawlers, hunted airborne plankton on the outer edges of the sky.

Meanwhile, as fox cubs played, and chicks fluffed up and fledged and became the bowel movements of magpies, and Theo's latrine began to smell like a rabbit's caecum, the universe not only expanded (meaning that everything got further away from us and from everything else), but the rate of that expansion increased (meaning that the universe got lonelier faster over the summer, and that the loneliness will continue to increase for ever).

Theo continued to sit, in the patch, in the sun, thinking of the petals, fuelled by molecules from an acre of land at the edge of the Severn Sea.

'I've found the secret!' he told himself. 'Unqualified, complete in-habitation. It doesn't matter so much what you inhabit: it might be a wood, a woman, or your breath. The key is to say: 'This is it! Here I am! Here and nowhere else! Now! Hwaet! Om! Cheers! Huzzah for the good ship Existence and all who sail her merrily onto the rocks of the next bloody moment!'

And then suddenly the cuckoo was gone, and with it Theo's bor-rowed title to the patch.

Out in the bay, beating up and down, up and down, up and down, ignoring the wind, and waiting, was a big white bird: an armoured goose with a beak like a bayonet.

ᚥᚥᚥ

Anyone, of whatever species, would have seen much the same if they had watched Theo over the next month.

He mooched up and down the tide line with his old rucksack on his back, picking up whatever the sea gave him. Planks and nails; canvas from a marquee that still smelt of beer and cucumber; a Norwegian spruce that had been at the centre of a very grand and very unhappy Christmas; rope for oakum; paint - loads of it - and brushes stiff with algae. Everything he needed, in fact, but glazier's putty and red lead for the caulking. For he was building a boat.

Steve from the pub, wandering past the hut one afternoon, saw the skeleton of the boat up on trestles, and offered a hand, some oak beams, and some long brass screws. Theo firmly and superstitiously declined.

'What are you going to do with it?, asked Steve.

'Go for a bit of a sail', said Theo.

ΨΨΨ

Anyone, of whatever species, would have seen, too, that Theo behaved differently on his boat-building days. It is best described as
moral hygiene. He drank only water, ate no rabbits, washed carefully
in the sea before he picked up his hammer, intoned the Trisagion,[58]
and slept on the ground rather than his mattress.

A caique grew up and out of the sea: big-bellied and generous; a
cabin that could take a curled man; a well in the bottom to keep live
fish; a stout stubby mast with a square sail; fertilizer sacks of rocks
for ballast; flare for cutting through the short steep seas of the
Aegean; a merry little boat in fairground colours, christened with
the blood of a broken-winged gull.

There was still no putty or red lead to be had, and he had to walk
into town for them.

Rachel

We were driving to the chip shop and I saw Theo at the side of the
road. I shouted at him and banged on the window and dad hooted
the horn but Theo didn't look up at all. He was walking really fast
and was thin and had a hole in his jumper.

Dad said that someone had told him that Theo was selling his motorbike and mummy said that was sensible because motorbikes are
really dangerous.

Eel

Under the rock the big old eel shivered. The morning's tide had brought a frond of Sargasso weed, and now an itch was spreading inside her abdomen.

The Author

The rest of the story comes from police reports and pure surmise.

There were no goodbyes, except to Rachel, who got a tattered post card with some illegible words.

The last communication I had from him was his written response, which I've reproduced above, to my latest notes about him. I'd got into the habit of showing my notes to him. Usually he'd just read and laugh and respond., and I'd rush home and try to remember what he'd said, but lately (since the events of Chapter 9, in which the dolphin nudged Theo's chest, trying to tell him about the bullet) he'd taken to writing to me on sheets of paper ripped from an exercise book. Several pages became exhibits at the inquest.

He went blithely. Everyone agreed on that. The last words anyone remembered him saying were about afterlife journeys in Egyptian and other mythologies. 'They must be terrifying for sedentary people', he had told Steve, apropos of absolutely nothing. These words nudged the coroner towards a psychiatric conclusion.

ΨΨΨ

He went at the end of the tangled times, before the swallows. He had been waiting for a spell of easterlies, and they swept him, the white bird, and two dolphins, fast and hard past Devon, and past the Lizard.

He steered well clear of the Scilly reefs, and was nearly crushed at night in the Bay of Biscay by a tanker that crept up on him when he was dozing. He woke up gagging from the halitosis of its bilges and saw only a deeper darkness than the sky and heard a clanging and a throb that filled his throat, and he wrenched the tiller round and the tanker throbbed on to Swansea.

The wind was kind enough. In a week he was at a Coruña, and then, worried about Atlantic westerlies skewering him on the rocks of northern Spain, headed a hundred miles offshore before turning south.

As he turned, a big eel that had travelled under the boat hung in the water for a moment, eyeing the keel, then dived to the deep blue cold, and swam slowly off to the west.

This was a sea without mood or age. It did not choose. It did not listen to supplicants. It simply *did*. And it always did. It heaved, hollowed out its own belly and sucked itself in. Its depths could become its top without any change in colour, yet it could change from white to black in a terrible moment. It could give with a crash or take away with a whisper. It could not be pitied - as even a mountain, doomed to erosion, can be pitied - and that is a frightening thing. It creaked, but it was not the creak of failing joints, but the creak of a workshop and a breaking yard. There were plenty of persons in the sea, but their personality never lent personality to the sea itself. A wood is a person; its animals are persons. Wood and animals take some of their personality from one another. But the sea is never, ever a person.

The dolphins bounced along in the bow wave, sometimes nuzzling the boat. A basking shark scraped alongside. Theo slept with his ear pressed against the hull, and the planks thrummed with the songs of whales. On dark clear nights, off Portugal, stars reflected in the water. There were stars above and below and all around: the boat was a star ship. Bioluminescence set the dolphins on fire, and when Theo poured his slop overboard, a blazing faecal comet spiralled down to a hagfish that was eating a cod from the inside.

The bird was always there, usually at the edge of vision. It was just as well, for Theo had no compass, no quadrant, no marine chronometer, and, probably, no plan.

His face burned in the wind. His mind followed his eyes to the horizon, and neither his eyes nor his mind could focus on a book. He guessed he was off the Costa Vicentina, and remembered eating goose barnacles in the sand dunes with a farm girl who tasted of samphire. But this was no longer a personal memory. It was merely a fact; something in an archive.

Suddenly the bird turned east. It left Theo as the boat wallowed and strained in the Straits of Gibraltar.

ΨΨΨ

Some say that the Mediterranean is a manageable, man-sized sea. Almost a gentle, gracious tutor of a sea; a district of Constantinople or Carthage.

It is not so, though on an August afternoon it can be easy enough to believe it. It is far safer to see the August afternoon as the cheese baiting a breakback trap. Unlike the Atlantic, the Mediterranean seems to have a face - with the Archaic smile of those icy *kouroi*. So perhaps one *can* appeal to the Mediterranean. Certainly men — though perhaps not women - have thought so. If it is so, it is all the more cruel, for then the sea has agency and ears, and yet chooses to behave as it does.

Theo hugged the north coast now, avoiding the marinas (which he couldn't afford), eating fish hauled up and dumped in his fish-well, and rice cooked in sea-water, and washing occasionally with water caught in a corner of the sail. Sometimes he'd run the boat aground and fearfully, his eyes turned down in the hope of avoiding contact or news, buy fuel for his stove.

The boat was red and his throat was rough with sand. Sometimes a high fast wind carried a carpet of musty green scent from writhing vegetative Africa and laid it over him as he slept and steered. He swung out towards Morocco because Spain was full of English.

ΨΨΨ

Throughout the Mediterranean, hiding under trapdoors in the flat calm, or in deep throated caves that lead down to the Styx, or sitting with their feet up in bars, there are demonic storms. This hysterical, personifying language is unavoidable. In half a minute they can drain all visibility from a world where, before, you could see well into another continent. Or spin the boat like a roulette wheel, or pull it down, or pick it up and shuffle it alongside other boats or houses or whales, or fling it like a cricket ball at a granite wicket.

Theo was suddenly in the water, blind and sick and dizzy, hurtling towards Africa with no sense of movement. The Christmas tree mast snapped; there was a roar alternating with silence like a huge heart; the sail went off into the Sahara.

After an age there was a crunch, and blackness, and then again a nudge, nudge, nudge against his side, and pebbles under his feet.

It does not matter much where he was. There were now no coordinates of any kind in heaven or earth or under the earth.

ΨΨΨ

The boat had survived, and was washed up next to him, though all
the charts were gone. A brand new mast, with a brand new sail, lay
on the beach. It took a day to fix it up, and another day to steel himself to relocate a finger that was out of joint, and another day to
sleep, and another day to recover from sleeping, and then another
night, looking into the dark under the falling waves: the deepest dark
there is, darker than the space between Neptune and the Pleiades;
dark with age and appetite and the absence of kindness; and then
he was off again, sailing always into the dawn, his skin alive with
pain. The sea always finds you out. If you've a cut on your face, or
an overblown nose, or a graze on your genitals, it'll tell you.

He came, I think, into Greek waters. I think he landed, insofar as
you can land in Greece. There is nowhere in Greece that's inland.
In fact nowhere in the world has been or will be inland for long.
There are marine molluscs on mountains, and our only future is salt.

He would have sat on the beach and listened, as he always did. Because nowhere in Greece is inland, the whole country murmurs.
Sounds that would be sharp-edged in England (bird song; the
shrieks of warring children) are smoothed by the sea into a sigh or
a hum.

.

He would have landed near to some reminder of Roman torture.
On every Greek promontory – especially those at the edge of the
sea – there's at least a cross, or a sacred pile of stones, or a chapel.
It's saying - whether delusionally or truly - that at the edge of the
chaos – where the view is only of the void – there is a Jonah's whale
waiting to take us through the depths and disgorge us on the other
side.

And then, I think, he set out again.

At the far end of the Mediterranean, as far as you can get from the churning sluice of Gibraltar, the sea is tired. It is always tired here: the flatness that seems like concavity is always here. Just sometimes, for the sake of some old pride, it puts on a show and smashes a boat or two, or drowns some children. But even then it is concave under the spume and the fury.

It was into this concavity that Jonah fell. The Jonah project was a joint venture between a desert god and the sea. It's interesting that Poseidon co-operated. You'd have thought he'd be too proud, or at least that he'd have negotiated a proper price for his co-operation. Perhaps he did.

The sea has not only stopped smiting; it's stopped *watching*. Perhaps it's decided that there's too much watching round here anyway. There are eyes in every spiky bush and every stone. But I don't think it is anything so considered. I think it's just tired. The big fish rotate more around their longitudinal axis here than in the rest of the world, though it's hotter – much hotter – than at the Atlantic end. Though their metabolic motors are racing, they themselves, as whole organisms, *sidle*.

ᛉᛉᛉ

I do not know what happened to Theo. It is neither my business nor my duty to know. I do not know what or whom he thought the white bird was, but I can guess. There were so many times when I thought his story was done; that he had suffered enough to win the right to rest; that he knew enough to be getting on with; that his mum's cooking was keeping him content, and that his dad had taught him how to swing the *komboloi* so as to calm him down when he started to over-think. But there was always more with Theo: problems that the rest of us couldn't see, or chose not to see: different ways that the world could be turned so that things looked different and had to re-evaluated from scratch. I do not know if that was bravery or integrity or plain pathology. And perhaps he did not find his mother and his father, as I had thought he did.

If I am pressed for a eulogy, all I can say is that he refused to take his morality from the ichneumon or from a cannibal that sicks up its young in a ball, that his bone marrow saved a Kurdish child, and that he has more right to use personal pronouns than I have.

ΨΨΨ

The hollow body of a one-eyed gull, now grey and spongy, washed up on the beach below Theo's old hut on the little brown sea. Unless change is itself a tragedy, there was no tragedy in this.

And the sea gave up the dead which were in it...;
And I saw a new heaven and a new earth:
for the first heaven and the first earth were passed away;
and there was no more sea.[59]

AUTHOR'S NOTE

This is a book about the sea.

I'm interested in what it means to live well.

I am interested in the sea because it is a large part of the world, and has generated me, and so has to be taken into account in deciding what the world is like, and what sort of creature I am, and therefore how a creature such as I am can be properly alive.

There is a trite saying in ethics: Good ethics demand good facts. It is an assertion that in order to live rightly, we need to have correct information about the world.

This is very worrying, for humans are in epistemic crisis, which generates identity crises and other psychological crises, which in turn fuel the epistemic crisis. It's terrible. Ever since Einstein – no, ever since Human A standing on a termite mound got a different view of the wildebeest than Human B standing on a pile of rocks – we've known that our account of reality depends on where we're standing. And on other things, such as whether Human A happened to have her eyes open, and on all the cognitive biases of all the witnesses called to testify, and on the weather and on what everyone had for lunch, and so on and so forth.

Can we really know anything – let alone sufficient to make satisfactory (let alone *right*) decisions about anything at all?

The epistemic crisis is psychologically crippling. No one knows much about themselves. And that not only makes us frightened and frightening; it also lays the foundation for further epistemic crisis. For if we know nothing about ourselves as observers, how can we say anything about what we observe?

To say something correct about a human being is a big ask. It's perhaps a lesser ask to see if we can say something correct (or at least less obviously incorrect than usual) about a small muddy bay on the Bristol Channel. The trouble with that, though, is that the bay is on the *sea*.

The epistemic crisis is expressed at many levels. One of the most basic, and hence most repercussive, is in relation to the senses. We choose to be woefully unsensual animals.

Everyone agrees that we have at least five senses. That is plainly a gross underestimate. But, by and large, we use only one: sight. It's an unfortunate choice. Any of the other four conventional senses would have been better.

I've never seen a tree. That's sad.

If I walk into a wood I get, for a fraction of a second, some visual data about the tree in front of me. A millisecond later I have translated those data into my *thoughts* about the tree. Those thoughts will bear almost no relationship at all to the tree. The real tree, I'm sure, is far more interesting, colourful, and charismatic than my thoughts about it. My thoughts about the tree are woven from twisted memories of other trees; of half-remembered fragments of poems about trees; of generic crap; of cosy abstraction.

This doesn't happen so readily with smells or sounds or touch or taste. My visually triggered thoughts are disastrously personal. Visually mediated thought is pure cognitive masturbation. I'm an insufferable narcissist: I see and regard nothing but my own thoughts: I'm self-referential and self-reverential: I get off on my own abstractions. I'm also (which is even worse), *wrong* about the way the world is. I'm an epistemic pauper. My thoughts about the world are not the world.

Even if my cognition didn't distort, and even if there were only five senses, and even if my eyes were fully open, I'd still be using only $1/5^{th}$ of the available information about the tree. Just think how well you'd get on if you made decisions about relationships or business or physics on the basis of 20% of the available data.

We are getting the whole world *wrong*. It shows.

If we want to know how to live properly in, say, a muddy bay on the Bristol Channel, we should try to perceive, as accurately as we can, what that muddy bay is like. If we don't know what a place is like, we're unlikely to be able to inhabit it as intensely, and therefore as satisfactorily, as we should.

In deciding what any place is like, or the facts of any event, it's best to call as many witnesses as possible.

Look at anything: a cup, say, or a road traffic accident. Move round it. The view changes, doesn't it? Which view is correct?

If you're interested in ethics there's a further complication. Ethics is about relationships with other entities. If it's hard to know anything about a tree, how can you know anything about the entities to which you owe the most stringent moral obligations? How can you know how to behave properly towards them?

Look around you. There are probably people – at least in your mind's eye. There are certainly non-bipeds. Inside the heads of each of them is a universe – a universe exhilaratingly inaccessible to you. The exploration of these universes is far, far harder, far, far more exciting, and far, far more worthwhile than the exploration of any distant galaxy. Unless you make some progress in that exploration, you can't behave decently.

But perhaps this is too ambitious. Humans are complex. Let's get back to trees and bays and other less demanding epistemic subjects. If an author *sees* perfectly - getting that uncontaminated one fifth of the available information about the bay - he'll be getting information only from the viewpoints at which he'd stood – looking down colonially on the bay from eyes stuck on the end of a bipod about five feet from the sand. If he moves only slightly – a foot to the left or right, or a couple of inches down – he'll have a completely different set of visual perspectives, and he'll have to start describing all over again.

Then suppose that he tries describing what he's smelt or heard from his one smell-point or hearing-point. It'll be a much longer description. Then suppose he moves his ears or his nose a few feet, and picks up his pen again....You get the idea.

Now remember that he is only a human, and only one human.

Non-human senses are very different. If I'd thought they were always, inevitably, unimaginably different, I couldn't and wouldn't have written lots of the things that I have.[60] But I take it that non-human perspectives are worth recording. We can argue about whether they are better or worse than human perspectives, but it's unarguably true that lots of perspectives are better than a few.

If we can get a more than usually accurate view of that muddy bay, we can then return to that trite observation about ethics, and begin to ask, with the benefit of a few more facts (or, rather, with the benefit of some facts perceived rather less unsatisfactorily than usual), what it means to live well in that bay.

All this epistemic uncertainty makes ludicrous the traditional distinction between fiction and non-fiction. I therefore make no apology for blurring it. The apology is needed from those who seek to maintain the distinction. Anyone who thinks they can write pure fiction lacks self-knowledge. Anyone who thinks they can write pure non-fiction doesn't know the subject well enough to be published. And to anyone who asks me what's fact and what's fiction, I can say, with complete honesty, that I haven't the faintest idea.

This is a story about a place and some creatures. It is a story because everything said about anything is necessarily a story. It is a story about a place because everywhere is a place, and every story has to happen somewhere.

And it is a story about creatures because Bishop Berkeley may have been onto something,[61] and places might not exist unless there's something to perceive them, and because places shape creatures, and creatures shape places, and so to attempt any discussion of causes has to deal both with creatures and places, and not to deal with causes is boring and cowardly.

Place secretes creatures. Creatures secrete place.

Most books about the sea are big, swirling, swaggering, blue-grey books, driven on by full sails creaking like trusses. They look down at the sea from a crow's nest in a satellite.

That's dangerous. It's asking for trouble. To write at all is presumptuous. To write about the sea is deadly blasphemy. There's something big and nasty out there that won't like it.

So in fear I have made this a little, brown book about a little, brown place. It looks out at the sea when it is barely sea – where it has only just got its salt; where it is a soup of English and Welsh soil; where, I hope, it won't have the confidence to destroy me.

It tries to be local. There's an ungeographical and unmetaphysical silliness about this, of course, because the sea is never local. It binds the world; it's the universal soup from which everything came, and in which everything is suspended, and in which everything subsists, but (as a gesture of humility to appease earth-shaking Poseidon), I need to say that it's even more ridiculous to seek to wrap my head around a Pacific reef than around a Somerset kelp bed. I'm best sticking to piers and wet gulls and bags of chips and cold pebbles and the rasp of sand on a February night.

'All names fall short of the shining of things', wrote Andrew Harvey.[62] Even the little brown things and little brown places shine so brightly that my retinas are burned and I'm struck blind. Which isn't a great start if you're writing a book that contains description.
In fear, and out of a number of superstitious and epistemological convictions, this little brown book tries be simple reportage. Surely, I thought, even the Earthshaker wouldn't kill a journalist for noting what the sources had said? Any anger should be directed to the sources themselves. It's ungodlike to shoot the messenger.

I grew up about as far inland in England as it's possible to get. And yet I had a sea all around me. I think we all have. Waves of dark heather crashed and foamed on my suburban beach, where the streetlamps began to give up. The wild roared and shuddered. Entropic tides of wilderness surged in and out of the driveway, leaving strange things stranded, wriggling and dying on the wrack line.

This metaphorical sea did the real sea's job for a while. It would do so still, had I not got on a bus to Scotland.

I've admitted that I don't know where true story ends and fable begins, any more than I know where the land ends and the sea begins. I do not know this even (or perhaps particularly) for any element of my own story.

AFTERWORD

I was in North Devon. I'd finished writing this book. I re-read some of the Author's note – all about the dangerous hubris of writing about the sea, and about how the sea is out to get us. It seemed hysterical, but it was too late to change it: the book was built on those ideas.

That afternoon I went swimming in the sea at a place that I know and love. I often swim there. It's a small bay about a mile's walk from the road.

I'd had my swim, and was walking out. I was knee deep in the water. There was a groan behind me, and then a roar, and a wave about the size of a house was coming for me. Running was hopeless: it was travelling far too fast. So I tried to dive through it. I had nowhere near enough momentum. The wave threw me about fifty yards. I was completely submerged. I knew there were rocks ahead, and was trying to protect my head with my arms. I was hurled onto a rock, and felt my leg break. Then the sea sucked me out again. I'm not sure how long I was out to sea, but another wave dumped me far enough up the beach for bystanders to pull me out of the surf. 'Dad must have been in that second wave', my sister later suggested. She's a woman not given to whimsy, fancy or sentiment, and she knew nothing of what had happened to Theo in that Athenian taverna opposite the demolition site.

Two hours later, after a lot of morphine, a lot of gas and air, and some spectacular out of body experiences, a helicopter winched me out. A clever surgeon later screwed me back together.

That rock would have cracked my head like an eggshell, snapped my neck like a twig, or burst my spleen like a blueberry. I am amazingly blessed and grateful to be alive. I have left the text as it was.

ACKNOWLEDGEMENTS

Every sentence of every book, just like every sentence spoken with our mouths, is plagiarized. Bibliographies are pointless: an honest bibliography would include everything the author had ever read.

Where I have plundered consciously from other books I have acknowledged it in the text or in a footnote. Many other writers have certainly seeped in. Adam Nicolson and Philip Hoare write more powerfully about the sea than any other living writers I know. The sea is deafening in Dylan Thomas, always audible in Dickens (despite his frock coat) and Shakespeare (although Stratford is about as far as you can get from the sea in England), and a leading character in absolutely everything written in Greek from whatever period.

I have known many seas, but supremely and formatively seas in Scotland, North Yorkshire, Somerset, North Devon, Cornwall, Dorset, west Wales, Ireland, Portugal, and Iceland. And far above all, Greece. Always I have encountered the careful, cheerful kindness of those who go down to the sea in ships, kayaks, or wet suits.

Jim Brooke-Jones, an expert boat-builder at Portsmouth's Historic Dockyard, was hugely helpful and hospitable. I sailed through the Aegean with Costa Pilavachi, and he helped greatly in reconstructing Theo's voyage from England to the eastern Mediterranean. Much of this book was written at Katerina Stathatou's house on Kythira, looking out over the sea towards Crete. I suspect, though I cannot be sure, that Theo sailed just to the north of Antikythira.

Many wise, shrewd, warm friends have helped to steer this book to harbour. It's invidious to pick out names, but I have to mention David Abram, Janice Armstrong, Theodoros Bargiotas, Manolis Basis, Melina Dritsaki, Steve Ely, Cal Flyn, Jay Griffiths, Caspar Henderson, Ben Hill, Helen Jukes, Paul Kingsnorth, Marinos Kyriakopolous, Andy Letcher, John Lister-Kaye, Helen Mort, Iain McGilchrist, Nigel McGilchrist, George Monbiot, Metaxia Pavlakou, Nigel and Janet Phillips, Keith and Emily Powell, Klara Segnoe, Margarita Thomakou, Peter Thonemann (who named the Greek and Turkish newspapers), Martin Shaw, Rupert Sheldrake, John Stathatos, Mark and Sue West, and Rob Yorke.

All the good parts of Theo's pub – and none of the bad – are based on the magnificent Pebbles Tavern in Watchet. If for some reason you wanted lager there they would serve it to you with a welcoming smile, but you really should go for the cider. No one gets their nose broken there, and so far as I know they don't trade lobsters for strippergrams. They are most certainly not xenophobic, sexist, or in any other way less than excellent. And Watchet is far from a grey, shit-stained little town.

None of my colleagues at the University of Oxford behaves remotely like Theo's. My own experience of the Academy has been, almost without exception, the direct opposite of his. I'm privileged to work with people who are interested in big questions, and only in little questions insofar as they illuminate the big ones. They have a deep suspicion of footnotes and loathe academic toadyism.

A central premise of this book is that the greater the number of perspectives, the better the view. Dolphins, crows and daughters are crucial co-authors. And so is James St Clair Wade, whose brillliant illustrations clairvoyantly expounded to me many of my own half-formed thoughts about how things should look.

My fantastic agent, Jessica Woollard, always believed in this book when there was no reason at all to do so. That meant and means such a lot.

And that brings me to my editor, Nadia Kingsley. It goes without saying that you've got to be mighty audacious and brave to take on a strange book like this. But, to boot, she's immensely kind, clever, efficient and acute. Her perceptive editing has made this a much better book. Thank you!

It's traditional for authors to thank their families fulsomely. I couldn't care less about the tradition: my family really have borne the brunt of all the briny absences and brackish moods. Mary, Lizzie, Sally, Tom, Jamie, Rachel, and Jonny: you're amazing, and I am so very grateful.

---

[1] *Moby Dick,* Chapter 23.

[2] E.g. at the end of Aeschylus' *Oresteia,* when the whole social order represented by the Chorus is swept away.

[3] Revelation 20:13, 21:1

[4] Genesis 1:20-25

[5] Genesis 1: 1-2

[6] See Carl Safina, *Beyond Words: What animals think and feel* (Picador, 2016)

[7] Being selfish and isolated is cognitively very cheap: you don't need a big brain. But in terms of fitness it's not recommended. Big, expensive, relationship-powering brains turn out to be very good value.

[8] See Gordon H. Orians, *Snakes, Sunrises, and Shakespeare: How evolution shapes our loves and fears* (University of Chicago Press, 2014)

[9] A reference to the (controversial) 'Aquatic Ape' theory, summarised at http://www.primitivism.com/aquatic-ape.htm

[10] There are, broadly, three evolutionary explanations of (apparent) altruism: kin selection (where x behaves altrustically towards y because y shares sufficient genes with x to make x's sacrifice for y worthwhile): reciprocal altruism (where x behaves altruistically towards y, expecting y to reciprocate to a degree that makes x's altruism worthwhile); and group selection (where x makes some sacrifice which will benefit the group of which x is a member).

[11] The Sargasso Sea

[12] The oldest recorded specimen of the European eel, *Anguilla anguilla,* was 88 years old.
http://genomics.senescence.info/species/entry.php?species=Anguilla_anguilla

[13] Jonathan Balcombe, *What a fish knows* (Scientific American, 2016)

[14] The Coriolis effect may have a slight effect on the direction in which water goes down a hole: see https://www.scientificamerican.com/article/can-somebody-finally-sett/

[15] Ketamine is routinely used for cat spays and castrations: there must be millions of cats out there who've had life-changing out-of-body experiences.

[16] Greek worry beads

[17] The idea that a material thing that we see is a more or less inadequate reflection of a non-physical 'form' or 'type' of that thing: see

https://plato.stanford.edu/entries/plato/

[18] Gregory Palamas (c 1296 – c 1359) would have been particularly helpful. Pseudo-Dionysus the Areopagite (late 5th-early 6th century) would have been useful too, though probably a few years later.

[19] Female followers of the Greek god Dionysus (who became the Roman god Bacchus).

[20] Nicomachean Ethics Book 1

[21] Countess of Feversham, *Strange stories of the chase: Foxhunting and the Supernatural,* Geoffrey Bles, 1973

[22] Denise L. Herzing, *Dolphin Diaries,* St. Martin's Press, 2011, pp. 31-32: cited Carl Safina, *Beyond Words: What animals think and feel,* Souvenir Press, 2016, pp. 363-64

[23] Safina, ibid, pp 67-69

[24] I wonder if Theo was thinking of Alan Garner's *Elidor* (William Collins, 1965)

[25] *The Spell of the Sensuous:* Vintage, 1996

[26] C.S. Lewis, *Surprised by Joy,* Geoffrey Bles, 1955

[27] 'And God blessed them, and God said unto them, Be fruitful, and multiply, and replenish the earth, and subdue it: and have dominion over the fish of the sea, and over the fowl of the air, and over every living thing that moveth upon the earth.' Genesis 1: 28 (KJV)

[28] I'm sure he'd have taken Mircea Eliade's , *Shamanism: Archaic Techniques of Ecstasy* (Princeton University Press, 2004) and, of the Joseph Campbell canon, at least *The Masks of God,* 4 vols: (1) *Primitive Mythology*; (2) *Oriental Mythology*; (3) *Occidental Mythology*; (4) *Creative Mythology* (Secker & Warburg, 1960), and *The Way of the Animal Powers,* vol. 1 of *Historical Atlas of World Mythology* (Harper & Row, 1983), and *The Way of the Seeded Earth,* vol. 2 of *Historical Atlas of World Mythology* (Harper and Row, 1989)

[29] The notion of the 'is-ought' fallacy, identified by David Hume, is the idea that it is illegitimate to make evaluative conclusions (typically, but not necessarily, of a moral nature) from mere facts: see https://plato.stanford.edu/entries/hume-moral/#io

[30] For an accessible summary of the science, see Bruce Hecker, 'How do whales and dolphins sleep without drowning?' https://www.scientificamerican.com/article/how-do-whales-and-dolphin/

[31] Thomas I.White, *In Defense of Dolphins: The New Moral Frontier,* (Wiley-Blackwell, 2007). Cited Philip Hoare, *The Sea Inside* (Fourth Estate, 2013),

pp. 173-74)

[32] Since antiquity there have been stories of dolphins rescuing humans. For discussion, see Carl Safina, *Beyond Words,* ibid, pp. 371-374.

[33] See Rachel Carson, *The Edge of the Sea,* (Houghton Mifflin 1955)

[34] See Milton Brener, *Faces: The changing look of humankind* (University Press of America, 2000); cp Iain McGilchrist, *The Master and His Emissary: The divided brain and the making of the western world* (Yale University Press, 2009)

[35] 'Reinforcing and discriminative properties of music in goldfish', Shinozuka et al, Behavioural Processes (2013) 99; 26-33

[36] Sir Henry Newboldt (1862-1938): 'He fell among thieves'.

[37] The Greek sea god, Poseidon, is often known as the 'Earth Shaker'.

[38] Giorgos Seferis (1900-1971): one of the most famous modern Greek poets.

[39] A good illustration of (perhaps surprising) animal ability is the ability of sheep to recognise different human faces from two dimensional images: see 'Sheep recognize familiar and unfamiliar human faces from two-dimensional images'
Franziska Knolle, Rita P. Goncalves, A. Jennifer Morton R. Soc. open sci. (2017) 4 171228

[40] *The Old Margate Hoy*

[41] The colour and pattern of the Medicinal Leech (*Hirudo medicinalis*) was much admired by the Victorians.

[42] The 'melon' – a sort of acoustic lens, made of lipids, that concentrates ultrasound in cetaceans.

[43] 'Alzheimer's disease in humans and other animals: A consequence of postreproductive life span and longevity rather than aging', Gunn-Moore, Danièlle et al. Alzheimer's & Dementia: The Journal of the Alzheimer's Association (2018) 14(2); 195 - 20

[44] Toxoplasma: an intracellular parasite common in many species, but particularly notorious in cats.

[45] Charles Darwin wrote to Asa Gray on 22 May 1860: 'With respect to the theological view of the question; this is always painful to me — I am bewildered— I had no intention to write atheistically. But I own that I cannot see, as plainly as others do, & as I sh^d wish to do, evidence of de-sign & beneficence on all sides of us. There seems to me too much mis-

ery in the world. I cannot persuade myself that a beneficent & omnipotent God would have designedly created the Ichneumonidæ with the express intention of their feeding within the living bodies of caterpillars, or that a cat should play with mice.'

[46] Genesis 7:17-24

[47] Exodus 7: 19-20

[48] Exodus 14: 23-28

[49] Matthew 14: 22-36; Mark 6: 45-56; John 6: 16-21

[50] See the story of the Wedding at Cana: John 2: 1-11: the first recorded miracle of Jesus, in which he turns water to wine.

[51] Genesis 1: 20-25

[52] See, eg, 'Intersex in the clam *Scrobicularia plana:* a sign of endocrine disruption in estuaries?' B.S. Chesman and W.J. Langston (2006): http://plymsea.ac.uk/1540/1/Chesman_%26_Langston_Intersex_in_clams.pdf

[53] See Charles Foster: 'Eight expectations: Review of 'Other minds: the octopus and the evolution of intellligent life'.' Literary Review, March 2017

[54] Jean-Baptiste Lamarck (1744-1829) was a French naturalist best known for his belief that evolution preceded by way of the inheritance by offspring of characteristics acquired in the lifetime of the parents. His ideas were subsequently discredited, but have recently enjoyed a renaissance. The modern idea of epigenetics is concerned with the way that the expression of genes is determined by factors other than the sequence of the DNA – factors such as the environment. Genes can be 'switched' on or off, or their expression modulated in other ways. Genetic determinism is dead. The sequence of one's DNA is not the only important determinant of gene function – and accordingly gene mutation is not the only substrate on which natural selection can work. There is a much more influential conversation between genes and environment than was once thought.

[55] See, e.g., Joseph Stromberg, 'How human echolocation allows humans to see without using their eyes': Smithsonian Magazine, 2013: https://www.smithsonianmag.com/science-nature/how-human-echolocation-allows-people-to-see-without-using-their-eyes-1916013/

[56] See Jonathan Sacks, *Radical then, Radical Now* (Continuum, 2000)

[57] Gregory of Nazianzus (c 329-390) was Archbishop of Constantinople. See Oration 38:11

[58] Prayer used (especially) in Eastern Orthodoxy: 'Holy God, Holy Strong, Holy Immortal, have mercy on us.'

[59] Revelation 20:13, 21:1

[60] I'm thinking mainly here of *Being a Beast* (Profile: 2016: Picador: 2017)

[61] George Berkeley, 1685-1953: Irish philosopher who explored, inter alia, the idea that objects require, for their very existence, an observer. 'To be is to be perceived', he held. His philosophy is most accessibly summarised in a couple of limericks, the first by Ronald Knox, and the second probably by Knox too: 'There once was a man who said: "God/Must think it exceedingly odd/If he finds that this tree/Continues to be/
When there's no one about in the Quad.' The rejoinder is: 'Dear Sir, Your astonishment's odd/*I* am always about in the Quad/And that's why the tree/Will continue to be/Since observed by/Yours faithfully, God.

[62] *A Journey in Ladakh* (Flamingo, 1983)

Other publications from Fair Acre Press:

These Are The Hands: Poems from the Heart of the NHS
An anthology of poems by NHS workers, about the NHS, and for the NHS (all profits are donated to NHS Charities To-gether), edited by Dr Katie Amiel, and emergency poet/owner of the world's first poetry pharmacy: Deborah Alma. "A wonderful anthology to celebrate the NHS, which itself is the greatest poem a country has ever written" STEPHEN FRY "The very heart of who we are and what we are here for. An exciting and wonderful book" MICHAEL ROSEN

Fan-peckled: Twelve Old Shropshire Words in Poems and Pictures by Jean Atkin & Katy Alston
Fan-peckled is one of the old words of Shropshire. It was col-lected in the 1870s from the little towns of Wem and Whitchurch. It just means 'freckled'. For anyone who loves old words, or Shropshire. "This spells Shropshire for me. And Katy Alston's illustrations bear comparison with Ravilious and Ardizzone" KATHERINE SWIFT

Burke & Hare by Tom Wentworth
The script of the play that THE SUNDAY TIMES describes as "Fast, funny and ever so slighlty sick" about the infamous 'body-snatchers' of olde Edinburgh. "An absolute blast... Rapid, adept and funny" LIBBY PURVES

Woods River Road by John Sewell
Poetry collection. "A wonderfully erotic, earthy, pagan, vital celebration of sexual love and of the land" JOHN BURNSIDE

Beyond Spring: Wanderings through Nature by Matthew Oates

Shortlisted for both the BBC Countryfile magazine's best Country Book of the Year award and the Richard Jeffries award and listed by the guardian as one of the best Nature books of its year: it describes a sequence of wanderings through the natural world of England from spring's genesis through to summer's fulfilment and includes memorable quotes from the Romantic poets, the great Victorian and Edwardian nature writers and several of today's leading nature poets. "An exuberant celebration of the British countryside at its joyous, rampant best - interweaving natural and literary landscapes" BRETT WESTWOOD "Beautiful and brilliant" PATRICK BARKHAM

I once knew a poem who wore a hat by Emma Purshouse and Catherine Pascall Moore

Winner of the International Rubery Award for Poetry "Emma's poems are full of life and laughs, bubbling with music and wisdom and silliness and jokes and cute animals. The book is crammed with tips to help the reader become a performer too." A.F.HARROLD "A useful, fun addition to poetry shelves and resources" THE SCHOOL LIBRARIAN JOURNAL

What not to wear in bed by Selima Hill

12 poetry sequences, in pamphlet form: released one a month through 2022 – by the Forward-prize, T.S Eliot and Whitbread prize-winning poet, Selima Hill. "The delight, surprise, and attack of Selima Hill: an accumulation of miraculous acts of poetry." DAVID MORLEY "As you'd expect from Hill, there's a matchless clarity and honesty to every poem, and it's beautiful and terrifying." LUKE KENNARD "Selima Hill is like our very own Emily Dickinson, but quintessentially

herself and unique." PASCALE PETIT "Selima Hill, who always wakes up the language and stirs up our notions of emotional and social propriety, is up to her brilliant tricks once again. Compelling and salutary." FIONA SAMPSON

Offcumdens by Bob Hamilton and Emma Storr
A square format black & white photography and poetry book, both in paperback and hardback, about a complete love of Yorkshire by two so-called newcomers, or *offcumdens* as the locals say. "There's a space; a liminal space, a creative space, an adventurous space and a surprising space where words and images meet and this superb book celebrates that exciting space." IAN McMILLAN

Please don't trample us: we are trying to grow! by Steph Morris
A poetry pamphlet about the environment - both natural and human, in which we find ourselves. "A fine engagement between affection and refined outrage" DALJIT NAGRA

#MeToo: rallying against sexual assault and harassment, a women's poetry anthology
"This book contains the poetry of necessity and truth, exploding into the light, where it goddam belongs. Please read these poems and then decide in what order you want to 1) cry 2) march 3) scream with relief and recognition 4) grab a sword-pen and write your own" AMANDA PALMER "With each and every poet in this collective I say #metoo" JESS PHILLIPS

Aeschylus' Persians - in a new version by Kaite O'Reilly
"Persians is a beautifuly poetic version of Aeschylus' tragic play." THE POETRY SOCIETY "The language is modern, the world-music timeless, the rhythms ring with echoes of Eliza-

bethan drama" GILLIAN CLARKE

Diversifly - poetry and art on Britain's Urban Birds
"A celebration of the wild world just beyond our front doors" MATT MERRITT "Birds are a constant source of wonder. This same sense of wonder has been captured, so expertly, by the poets and artists in this book" BRETT WESTWOOD

Rescue from the Dark by Paul Francis
"This isn't just a collection of perfectly executed verse, nor is it just a wonderfully varied array of incisive poems that peer closely at those nuggets of history and newspaper clippings which have caught this poet's eye. This collection is important and urgent" EMMA PURSHOUSE

The Goldsmith's Apprentice by Keith Chandler
Winner of the International Rubery Award for Poetry. "A wonderful and generous book. The poems welcome you in and hold your attention with their deftness, attentiveness and joy-in-making" DAVID MORLEY "These poems are The Real Thing" JONATHAN EDWARDS

Milton Keynes UK
Ingram Content Group UK Ltd.
UKHW031822250824
447283UK00001B/16

9 781911 048701